MRS. JEFFRIES
REVEALS HER ART

G·K
Hall
&C°

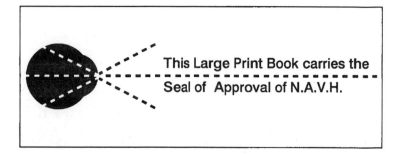

MRS. JEFFRIES

REVEALS HER ART

Emily Brightwell

G.K. Hall & Co. • Thorndike, Maine

Published in 2000 by arrangement with The Berkley Publishing Group, a member of Penguin Putnam Inc.

G.K. Hall Large Print Paperback Series.

The text of this Large Print edition is unabridged.
Other aspects of the book may vary from the original edition.

Set in 16 pt. Plantin by Minnie B. Raven.

Printed in the United States on permanent paper.

Library of Congress Cataloging-in-Publication Data

Brightwell, Emily.
   Mrs. Jeffries reveals her art / Emily Brightwell.
     p. cm.
   ISBN 0-7838-9104-0 (lg. print : sc : alk. paper)
   1. Jeffries, Mrs. (Fictitious character) — Fiction. 2. Witherspoon,
Gerald (Fictitious character) — Fiction. 3. Police — England —
Fiction. 4. Women domestics — Fiction. 5. England — Fiction.
6. Large type books. I. Title.
PR6052.R4446 M73 2000
823'.914—dc21   00-039598

MRS. JEFFRIES
REVEALS HER ART

Chapter 1

"I don't care what kind of a report you've had," Neville Grant snapped impatiently. "No one here knows that person. Now kindly take yourself away and don't bother me or my household again."

"I'm sorry to disturb you, sir," said Constable Theodore Martin — Teddy to his friends — swallowing nervously. Just his rotten luck that the master of the house himself would answer the door and not the ruddy butler. "But we must make inquiries. It's our duty. Are you sure none of your servants have seen this woman?"

Grant glared at the pale-faced lad who dared to continue questioning him. The fact that the man was a policeman didn't intimidate him in the least. "Are you deaf, young man? I've already told you. Some incompetent has made a mistake or, more likely, is playing the police for fools, which, by the look of you, isn't difficult to do. This household is hardly likely to be issuing invitations to women like that."

"We've still got to inquire, sir," the constable said quickly. "Someone's filed a report. She's gone missing. This house is the last known place where she was, sir. That's why we've got to make sure no one here's seen her."

"You've the wrong address." Grant stamped his cane against the parquet floor for emphasis. "She wasn't here. Now go away."

Martin hesitated indecisively. He didn't like to make a fuss, but if he went back to the station without even setting foot in the house, his sergeant would have his guts for garters. Ever since the ruddy Whitechapel killings, the police had to be extra careful — even if it was some flitty artist's model that had gone missing. More likely this old tartar was right — the woman probably hadn't come here at all. But if the missing girl turned up with her throat slashed or her guts torn out and the newspapers found out that the police hadn't even bothered to make inquiries when she'd been reported missing — Constable Martin didn't even want to think about that! "It is the right address, sir," he insisted.

Grant's wrinkled face reddened in rage. "How dare you contradict me," he yelped, stamping his cane again and coming within a hair's breath of smashing the constable's toe. "I don't care what address you've got." Grant started to close the door. "And I don't care if the girl has been kidnapped by white slavers. Someone's made a mistake. No one here knows anything about a missing woman."

"If I could just speak to the rest of the household, sir," Martin persisted desperately. It wasn't just his superiors he worried about facing if he went back without any information. It was that French woman. She'd raised such a ruckus down at the station this morning that even his hardened old sergeant had stepped back a wary pace or two when she was ranting and raving like a she-demon.

"Don't be ridiculous. We have guests this afternoon," Grant snapped. "I'm not having you bother my wife or anyone else with this silly matter."

"Then if I could have a word with your servants," the constable asked. "Maybe one of them invited her."

"My servants are hardly in the habit of inviting their friends for social calls."

"But one of them might know something."

"They've already been spoken to, you fool," Grant shouted, his complexion deepening to crimson. "The butler made inquiries amongst the staff yesterday after that other constable came round bothering us with this ridiculous tale. None of them know what the blazes you're on about either. You've bothered us twice now and we've been very patient. But enough is enough. Now get off with you and leave us in peace." With that, he slammed the door in Martin's face.

The constable sighed and trudged down the three steps to the paved walkway. As he went out the ebony wrought-iron gate that surrounded the property, he glanced back over his shoulder.

Blooming toffs, he thought as he glared at the handsome three-story brick house, just because they're rich they think they don't have to answer to the law. Well, they'd find out soon enough that they did. Constable Martin knew in his bones that this wasn't the end of things.

"Zhey do nothing!" Nanette Lanier banged her dainty fist against the tabletop hard enough to rattle the china. "She's been gone now for a week and still zhey do nothing. Zee English police," she cried. "Useless."

Mrs. Hepzibah Jeffries, housekeeper to Inspector Gerald Witherspoon of Scotland Yard, would normally have challenged such a statement, but considering the highly excitable state of her guest, she thought it best to let the comment pass.

"Miss Lanier," she began, only to be interrupted.

"Please call me Nanette."

"Very well, Nanette," she replied. She glanced at the clock. Almost three. The others should be back any moment. This would go a good deal easier if the rest of the staff were here. Smythe, the coachman, had taken everyone, even Mrs. Goodge, the cook, out for a drive in the inspector's carriage. "I quite sympathize with your position. I don't quite understand . . ." She paused, relieved, as she heard the back door open and the muted sound of several voices talking all at once. Good, the others were back. Now she wouldn't

10

have to deal with this on her own.

Nanette's expression of indignation turned to alarm. "Is zat zee inspector?" she asked.

"No, no," Mrs. Jeffries assured her. "It's the rest of the staff. They've been out this afternoon."

"I told ya you'd like it," Wiggins, the footman, exclaimed.

Mrs. Goodge, her hat somewhat askew and her spectacles slipping down her nose, bustled into the kitchen with Wiggins right on her heels. Fred, the mongrel dog the household had adopted, trotted in after them.

"Smythe drove too fast," the cook groused, but her round cheeks were flushed and despite her grumbling she was smiling. She stopped dead when she saw Mrs. Jeffries had a guest.

"He weren't goin' that fast," Wiggins said defensively. "Not like that time he made it all the way to the . . ." He broke off in mid-sentence as he spotted the beautiful woman sitting next to the housekeeper. He stumbled to his left to avoid ramming into the cook's broad back.

"Good afternoon," Mrs. Jeffries said calmly. "As you can see, we have a guest. This is Miss Lanier." She gestured at Nanette, who nodded politely. "Miss Lanier," she continued, "this is Mrs. Goodge, our cook, and Wiggins, our footman."

"Pleased to meet you," Mrs. Goodge said.

"Likewise," Nanette said with a regal incline of her head.

"Miss Lanier is joining us for tea," Mrs. Jeffries explained.

"I'll just put my hat away." Mrs. Goodge shot the housekeeper a curious look as she bustled off toward the hallway and her room.

Wiggins, who was still staring at the woman like a love-struck cow, started for a chair, tripped over his own feet, blushed bright red and then managed to seat himself without further ado.

"Where are Betsy and Smythe?" the housekeeper asked him. Nanette Lanier's arrival wasn't a social call. Mrs. Jeffries wanted everyone here before the woman went any further with her story. She forced herself to stay calm, deliberately keeping a tight lid on her rising excitement. She didn't want to get her hopes up. Nanette's problem might be a tempest in a teapot. But she hoped not. She hoped that soon the household would be out and about doing what they did best. Snooping. Seeking answers. Solving a mystery. They were very good at it too. But then, they should be. They'd done it often enough in the past. As the household staff for Inspector Gerald Witherspoon of Scotland Yard, they'd had plenty of practise. Not that their inspector had any inkling they regularly assisted him in his cases. Oh no, that would never do. But the point was, they did. Why, if not for them, their dear inspector would probably still be a clerk in the records room.

"They're just coming," Wiggins answered absently, his gaze still on their guest. He was the perfect picture of a love-struck youth. His eyes had gone all soft and dreamy, a half smile played around his mouth and a rosy blush had swept across his cheeks. Mrs. Jeffries ducked her head to hide a smile. Wiggins would be mortified when he looked in a mirror. Several tufts of his dark brown hair were sticking up at the back of his head.

The cook returned and took her regular chair at the table just as the back door opened again and the muted voices of the maid and the coachman drifted down the hallway. A moment later they came into the kitchen.

They made a striking contrast. Betsy, pretty and slender with blue eyes and blond hair, walked daintily next to a dark-haired hulk of a man. "Oh!" she exclaimed. "We've got company." She poked her companion in the arm. Smythe looked toward the table. His features were strong enough and brutal enough to intimidate a bear, but he'd not noticed they had a visitor because his eyes had been gazing adoringly at the maid.

Mrs. Jeffries repeated the introduction and then said, "Miss Lanier has come here for our help. It seems she has a problem." Her voice was calm and her expression serene, but there was something in her tone that caught all their attention.

Smythe's lips curved in a smile.

Mrs. Goodge grinned.

Betsy's eyes sparkled.

Even Wiggins jerked his gaze away from the Frenchwoman to look at the housekeeper in pleased surprise.

Mrs. Jeffries knew good and well what was going on in their minds. The same thing she'd thought when she'd opened the back door fifteen minutes ago and seen Nanette standing there. They had a case. A mystery to solve.

"What kind of a problem?" the cook asked eagerly.

"Before we go into that," Mrs. Jeffries said, "I'd like to remind everyone that Miss Lanier was involved in one of our first cases."

"But of course," Nanette said quickly. "It was when zat awful Dr. Slocum was murdered. I was working as a maid to Mrs. Leslie. We were Dr. Slocum's neighbors."

"It were that Knightsbridge one?" Wiggins exclaimed eagerly.

"Oui," Nanette replied, giving him a dazzling smile. "C'est correct. I remember, you see. I remember very well what I saw when zee police were trying to find out who killed Slocum. If it had not been for all of you, zee real killer would have gotten away with it. Zat's why I come here when zee police do nothing. I zink all of you are very good at finding answers."

No one was quite sure how to respond to her statement, so no one said anything. Save for the faint ticking of the carriage clock on the cupboard shelf, the room was silent as they all drifted back to the memory of the first case

14

they'd knowingly worked on together. It hadn't been their first case; there had been those horrible Kensington High Street murders. But on that one, they'd each worked separately, under Mrs. Jeffries's guidance and without even knowing what they were doing. But the murder of Dr. Bartholomew Slocum had been different. Mrs. Jeffries had realized they not only enjoyed and were good at snooping about but were just as devoted to the inspector as she was, and that they could work together as a team.

It had been the Slocum murder that had really brought them together. Mrs. Jeffries smiled at the memory. Now they were a family.

Misinterpreting the continued silence, Nanette quickly said, "I can keep a secret. If you help me, I won't say a word to anyone, especially not to your Inspector Witherspoon."

"Well," Mrs. Jeffries said thoughtfully, glad the woman had given them this promise freely, "that would put us more at ease. Now as to whether or not we can help you, we can't determine that until we know precisely what it is you need."

"My friend is missing," Nanette said. She plucked a pristine white handkerchief out of the pocket of her elegant green spring jacket and dabbed at her eyes. "She's been gone for a week."

Mary Grant's serene expression didn't change as she watched her husband come out the French doors and stamp across the lawn to

15

where she was entertaining his wretched business guests. Her eyes narrowed slightly as she saw Neville deliberately smash an early blooming daffodil with his cane. They'd discuss that later, she thought before casting her gaze back to their visitors. Tyrell and Lydia Modean weren't friends but business acquaintances. And though they'd been foisted upon her by her husband, she was far too proud a hostess to ever do less than her best. She smiled warmly at the tall man standing behind his wife, who was seated directly across from her. "Have you had time to visit many galleries?" she inquired politely. Modean was quite an attractive man, even if he was an American.

"Quite a number of them," Tyrell Modean replied. He laid a hand on his wife's shoulder. He'd been standing here now for ten minutes and was hoping they'd go in to tea soon. "We took in the Japanese Gallery on New Bond Street this morning. Some of the work was exquisite, wasn't it, Lydia?"

But it wasn't Lydia Modean who replied. It was the man sitting across from their hostess. James Underhill was also a guest, but one who'd been invited by Arthur Grant, Neville's son, who was slouched in a chair across the table. "Exquisite? Do you really think so?" Underhill said doubtfully. He opened a tin of mints and popped one in his mouth.

"Yes," Modean replied, not bothering to look at the Englishman. "I do." He deliberately moved so that he was turned away from Underhill. The snub was obvious to everyone seated at the table. Helen Collier, Mary Grant's sister, leveled an outraged frown at the American.

"Mrs. Grant," Modean continued calmly, "I understand the Caldararos were originally part of your family's collection."

Underhill shot a fierce glare at the American's broad shoulders. God, he hated him. He snapped the lid shut on his mints and started to put them back in his coat pocket.

"James," Mary ordered. "Could you go and get Mr. Modean a chair? Take Arthur with you to help carry it. They're quite heavy."

James Underhill was outraged. The witch was treating him like a servant. Well, by God, she'd pay for that. He glared quickly at the others around the table. Arthur practically trembled as Underhill's gaze raked him. Helen gave him her mewling calf's smile that for some odd reason she thought was attractive and Mary merely stared at him imperiously, daring him to object. Modean and his slut of a wife didn't even bother to look in his direction.

Underhill slapped the tin onto the table. "Of course, Mrs. Grant," he replied coldly. "I'll be delighted to get Mr. Modean a chair. Come along, Arthur. I could use a hand."

"Have you told the police?" Mrs. Goodge asked. Her tone was polite, but behind her spec-

17

tacles, her eyes were suspicious. She'd never had much liking for foreigners. Especially the French.

"Zee police!" Nanette snorted. "Useless fools! I went to them zee morning after Irene did not come home! Zhey claimed zhey'd make inquiries. But zhey did nothing. A rich man says he knows nothing of Irene and zhey are cowed like zee dog."

"I'm not quite followin' ya," Smythe said softly. "Why don't ya start at the beginnin' and tell us everythin'?"

"But I've already told Mrs. Jeffries," Nanette wailed. "I don't want to waste time. Something has happened to Irene. I know it. I can feel it in my liver."

"Liver?" Wiggins echoed. "That's a funny place to feel somethin'."

Nanette waved her hand impatiently. "Not my liver — what's zat other word . . ." She tapped her chest.

"Heart?" Betsy suggested.

Nanette nodded. "Zhat's it. I can feel it in my heart. Sometimes I get my English mixed up when I'm excited or upset and now I am very upset."

"Then I suggest you drink your tea and calm down," Mrs. Jeffries said. "You'll need to have all your wits about you when you tell us the facts of this matter."

Nanette nodded and took a deep breath. "But of course. You are right. I must be calm. It happened last week. My friend Irene Simmons came to take tea with me. A charming custom, is it not? Afternoon tea . . . but forgive me, I'm wandering off zee point. Irene lives in zee flat upstairs from my shop. She lives with her *grandmère*. Pardon, I mean grandmother."

"You own a shop?" Betsy asked curiously.

"A hat shop," Nanette replied proudly. "We carry all zee latest designs from Paris. We also carry a full line of gloves, scarves, fans and shawls."

"Go on," Mrs. Jeffries prompted. She too was curious how someone who only a few years ago was a lady's maid had acquired the capital to open her own business. But she wasn't going to ask that question now. She'd learned it was better to find some answers indirectly. "Do tell us about Miss Simmons."

"She's an artists' model," Nanette continued. "But Irene is a good girl, a decent girl. She is from a good family. They once had a bit of money, but when her parents died, she and her grandmother lost everything. I gave her a job working for me in zee shop . . ."

"I thought you said she was an artists' model," Wiggins asked.

"She is. But she only got her first modeling position a few months ago. A Spanish artist named Gaspar Morante happened to come into zee shop. He took one look at Irene and asked her to pose for him. He didn't offer her much money, but I told her to do it because I knew it might lead to other work. To be honest, my own business hadn't been so good."

"So she doesn't work for you now?" Smythe asked.

"Only occasionally," Nanette replied. "Her *grandmère* is quite ill. Irene needed to make money to pay for her medicines and zee doctor."

"So now she's makin' a livin' posin' for pictures?" Mrs. Goodge asked, her tone clearly indicating her thoughts on that kind of employment.

"She is a decent woman," Nanette declared with a sniff. "She does not pose in zee nude even though zat ridiculous Englishman offered her a hundred pounds."

Mrs. Jeffries reached over and patted Nanette's arm. "No one is saying your Miss Simmons isn't a perfectly nice woman . . ."

"That's right," Wiggins interrupted. "And even if she took all her clothes off, we'd still go out and look for her."

"Really, Wiggins," the cook snapped. "Please watch your tongue."

Wiggins blushed a fiery red. "Sorry. What I meant to say was that no matter what Miss Simmons does for employment, we'd look for 'er if she's missin'. No one deserves to be ignored just because they might be poor or different or . . . well." He looked helplessly at the housekeeper. "You know what I mean, Mrs. Jeffries."

"Of course we do, Wiggins, and I must say, you're absolutely right." She smiled approvingly at him and then turned to Nanette. "Do continue with your story. Miss Simmons came to have tea with you last week," she prompted.

"It was quite late in zee afternoon. Irene, she was excited because she'd received an offer of employment. She was to go zat night and discuss the terms with zee artist. I walked her to zee corner, to zee omnibus stop, and waited with her till it came. Zat was the last time I saw her."

"Do you know where she was going?" Betsy asked. "Do you have an address?"

"To a house on Beltrane Gardens. Zat's why Irene was so excited. The address was very fashionable, and she was sure she'd get a good wage," Nanette explained. "But she never came home. Zee next morning, her *grandmère* came down to zee shop and told me Irene's bed hadn't been slept in."

"What did you do?" Betsy asked.

"As I told you, I went to zee police. I was afraid there'd been an accident. But Irene, she wasn't in any of zee hospitals and zee police hadn't found any bodies without zee names."

"Huh?" Wiggins said.

"She means unidentified bodies," the housekeeper clarified.

"Zat's right. There were no unidentified bodies." Nanette pursed her mouth in disgust. "I even gave them zee address of zee house Irene went to, but zhey did nothing. Zee man who owns zee house told zem Irene never arrived. He is lying."

"Why do you think 'e's lyin'?" Smythe asked.

"Because I know Irene," Nanette declared. "I know she went to zat house. She needed zee work so badly she wouldn't have dared not gone. Zat's how I know he is lying . . . zat stupid old man. He's lying about Irene and zee police will do nothing . . ." Nanette broke off and launched into French with such speed and fury that everyone around the table was rather glad they couldn't understand what she was saying.

When the storm had passed, she got a hold of herself, wiped her wet eyes and said, "Please forgive me, but Irene is very dear to me, like a sister. I'm alone in zhis country. She and her *grandmère* aren't just my neighbors, but my family. I know zat Mr. Grant is lying. Why, he even claimed he hadn't sent zee note asking Irene to come. But he had sent it . . . I saw it with my own eyes."

"You saw it?" Mrs. Jeffries said. There were a dozen different explanations as to why the girl hadn't arrived at the house, but for now, they'd accept Nanette's assumption that the girl had indeed arrived at her destination that evening.

"*Oui*," Nanette cried, "and there is nothing wrong with my eyes. Irene did not write zat note to herself."

"So you're suspicious of this, er . . . Mr. Grant because you think he lied to the police," Mrs. Goodge said.

"He is lying! It was his notepaper. It had his name and address on it. Neville Grant. Thirty-four Beltrane Gardens, Holland Park."

Smythe sucked in his breath. "Cor blimey, that's right near 'ere."

"Does Irene have a sweetheart?" Betsy asked softly.

"*Non.*" Nanette shook her head. "There is no one. Several young men have been interested, but Irene is devoted to her *grandmère*. She would never desert her to run off with someone."

"Maybe somethin' 'appened to 'er after she left the Grant 'ouse?" Wiggins suggested. "You said yourself it were evenin'. Maybe somethin' 'appened to 'er after she come out?"

"I don't believe zat," Nanette said emphatically. "If she'd been there and gone, zhen why would zis man keep lying to zee police? He claims she was never there at all and I know she was."

"Perhaps someone was playing a trick on her?" Mrs. Jeffries suggested.

"I thought of zat," Nanette replied, "but zhen again, why wouldn't Grant admit she'd come to the door and zhey'd sent her off? But he said she was never there. I know she was. I saw her get on zee omnibus."

"That doesn't mean Irene didn't get off somewhere between the stop and the Grant house," Betsy pointed out. "Perhaps she stopped off to buy something at the chemist's?"

"Impossible," Nanette insisted. "She hadn't enough money."

"None at all?" Mrs. Goodge asked suspiciously.

"None." Nanette snorted delicately. "I had to loan her zee fare for zee omnibus. Zee next day, Madam Farringdon, one of my customers, came into zee shop. She mentioned zat she'd seen Irene on zee omnibus zee night before. Of course I questioned her, because I knew by zat time zat Irene hadn't come home. Madam said zat Irene and she had gotten off zee omnibus together and even walked up Holland Park Road. Madame left her at zee corner of Beltrane Gardens. That's only a very leetle distance from zee Grant house. What could have happened to Irene? It was a public street and she only had to walk a leetle ways to her destination."

"Had it gone dark by then?" Smythe asked.

Nanette nodded. "Yes, but when Madam Farringdon left Irene, she didn't have far to go."

" 'Ow was Miss Simmons plannin' on gettin' 'ome?" Wiggins asked.

Nanette shrugged. "I lent her money for a hansom. I didn't want her on zee streets too late at night. Why?"

"I was just wonderin'," he mumbled.

"Will you help me?" the Frenchwoman pleaded. "Her *grandmère* is frantic with worry, and so am I. I can pay you for your trouble."

There was an immediate chorus of protests. But it was Smythe's harsh tones that stood out. "We 'elp people because it's right, not because we're wantin' to make a bob or two."

"We're not a private inquiry firm." Mrs. Goodge sniffed.

"Please excuse me." Nanette's pretty blue eyes filled with tears. "I didn't mean to offend."

"None is taken," Mrs. Jeffries said calmly. There were a number of things to consider before they leapt into this venture. The main one being that they might not have any more luck in locating this poor woman than the police had. "But before we can agree to assist you, we really must discuss it among ourselves."

Nanette leapt to her feet. "I'll step outside in zee garden for a few minutes. Will zat give you enough time?"

Taken aback, Mrs. Jeffries could only nod. She'd rather thought they might have the whole evening to discuss the matter, but as Nanette was already scurrying toward the back door, there wasn't much she could do about it. She waited till she heard the door close before turning to the others. "What do you think?"

"We should 'elp 'er," Wiggins said quickly. "Poor lady's in a state, worryin' about 'er friend."

Mrs. Goodge sighed. "Well, it's not a murder," she began, "but finding this model is better than sittin' around here twiddling our thumbs."

"I don't know." Betsy glanced toward the back hall and shook her head. "We've never really done anything like this and if the girl's been gone a week . . ."

"You think she's already dead?" Smythe said bluntly.

"I'm not saying that," Betsy explained. "But there's something funny about the whole thing."

Mrs. Jeffries rather agreed with the maid's assessment. But she didn't want to give her opinion until everyone had been heard from. "Smythe, what do you think?"

Smythe leaned back and folded his arms across his massive chest. "Betsy's right. Somethin' strange is goin' on. But I don't think the girl's dead. I think someone's got 'er."

"You don't think she's dead? Goodness. Why?" Mrs. Jeffries was curious as to his reasoning.

"Because Nanette's already been to the police about this and even though she claims they ain't doin' nothin' about it, they probably are. Since this awful Ripper case, they're under a lot of pressure when it comes to missin' young women. Maybe they haven't brought this Grant feller in for questionin', but you can bet your last farthin' they're watching the morgues and the 'ospitals." Smythe shrugged. "Probably watchin' 'im, as well."

"What are you sayin'?" Wiggins scratched his chin.

"I'm sayin' 'er body 'asn't turned up," Smythe replied softly. "And there's not many places in a crowded city to hide a corpse."

"What about the river?" Mrs. Goodge put in quickly. "That's a good place to get rid of it."

Smythe shook his head. "It woulda floated up by now and someone would've seen it."

"So what do you think's happened?" Betsy prodded.

"I think she's been kidnapped," he said seriously.

Mrs. Jeffries wasn't sure she would go that far, but there was enough to Nanette's tale to warrant a further look. "What do you all think? Should we agree to help find this young woman?" She looked around the table at the others.

"I think we ought to," Betsy declared. "We can find out if she went into the Grant house if nothing else."

"I'm for it," Smythe agreed. "Mind you, I don't think we're goin' to have much more luck than the police . . ."

"Of course we will," Mrs. Goodge scoffed. "We've got ways of findin' things out that the police don't."

"That's true," Mrs. Jeffries murmured. They were quite good at digging out information. Even Mrs. Goodge, who never left the kitchen, could find out just about anything about anyone who was important in the city. But then, the cook had a veritable army of people marching through her domain. Tradesmen, delivery boys, costermongers, chimney sweeps and laundrymen. She kept them well supplied with sweet cakes and tea while she ruthlessly pumped them for every morsel of information there was to be had. "We're agreed, then. We're going to help?"

Everyone nodded. Wiggins got to his feet. "I'll just nip out and get Miss Lanier."

Mrs. Jeffries raised her hand. "Not yet. I think

27

we ought to bring the inspector into this."

"What for?" Mrs. Goodge demanded. "He'll not be able to do anything the police haven't already done."

"On the contrary. According to what Nanette told me earlier, a police constable has gone to the Grant house twice requesting information. They didn't even get inside the place."

"So what good would it do to get the inspector involved?" Smythe asked.

Mrs. Jeffries smiled. "Ah, but he's not a constable, is he? It's a far different matter when an inspector shows up on your doorstoop and starts asking questions. If nothing else, it will put the cat among the pigeons . . ."

Smythe chuckled. "I see what you're gettin' at."

"I don't," the cook demanded.

"Simple, Mrs. Goodge. If someone in that house knows anything about Irene Simmons, the inspector showin' up and askin' a few questions might loosen a few tongues."

"I say, Mrs. Modean is quite a lovely lady, isn't she?" Arthur Grant said to his companion as they paused at the top of the stairs and watched the couple below entering the drawing room.

James Underhill shrugged and patted the pocket of his elegant black jacket, checking to see that he had his box of mints handy. Damn, they were gone. He'd probably left them out in the garden earlier. "She's beautiful, but hardly a lady. She was a model before Modean married her. I ought to know. I'm the one who introduced them."

Grant gave Underhill a knowing smirk. "I fancy you wouldn't say something like that within earshot of her husband." He was satisfied when he saw a quick flush creep up Underhill's cheek. The man didn't like being reminded of their earlier meeting with the American. "Modean doesn't appear to like you very much."

"We've had dealings before," Underhill muttered. He started down the stairs, one well-manicured hand clasped lightly onto the polished mahogany banister.

"He seems a cultured sort, for an American." Arthur fell into step next to Underhill.

"Don't be absurd." Underhill stopped. His fingers tightened against the wood. "Modean's nothing. He's just a stupid, colonial upstart who thinks because he's made a bit of money he can buy art and culture the same way he buys mining shares or bonds. The man can barely read. No real education, no breeding, no family. Nothing but money. That's all they care about in America. Money." He continued down the stairs.

"Then it's fortunate for Modean that he has so much of it." Arthur said gleefully, taking such momentary delight in reminding Underhill of today's humiliation that he forgot Tyrell Modean and his American money were causing

29

him a lot of trouble as well. "But rather unfortunate for us," he amended quickly, hoping that Underhill hadn't quite realized he was deliberately trying to bait him. Sometimes, Arthur lamented, he frequently let his mouth loose without thinking.

Underhill was no fool. He shot Arthur a withering glare as they reached the bottom of the stairs. Across the wide hall, they could hear the muted voices of the others.

Arthur swallowed nervously and stepped back a bit. "Sorry," he mumbled. "I didn't mean . . ."

"Stop trying to goad me," Underhill warned. "You haven't the wit for it. In any case, without me, you're in very deep trouble. Don't forget that, my friend."

Grant's pale face turned even whiter. "But you will help me," he pleaded, casting a quick glance toward the drawing room. "He'll toss me out if he finds out. Yee gods, he'll probably kill me. You promised . . ."

"I promised nothing," Underhill interrupted. He was beginning to enjoy himself. The momentary shame at being reminded of Modean's snub was washed away as he saw Grant cringing like a whipped pup. "This really isn't my problem at all, is it?"

"It will be if it all comes out," Grant blustered, his hazel eyes shifting between the drawing room and the man standing in front of him. "If I go down, you go down."

"Do you really think he'll believe you?" Un-

Chapter 2

Inspector Gerald Witherspoon hoped he was doing the right thing. He slowed his pace as he walked up Holland Park Road. Perhaps he ought to have sent Wiggins or Smythe over to fetch Constable Barnes? But as the constable was off duty, he hadn't wanted to bother him at home. Especially for something like this. So he'd decided to bring his coachman and footman along with him — unofficially, of course.

Still undecided, because what he was doing was highly irregular, Witherspoon stopped in the middle of the pavement. His two companions stopped as well.

"Is somethin' wrong, Inspector?" Smythe inquired politely.

"No, no. I just needed to have a bit of a think. Was Miss Lanier absolutely certain of the address?" he asked. Perhaps he ought to have sent Miss Lanier to the police station, but she'd been so desperate, so distraught. He really hadn't had the heart to refuse her request. Especially when she'd gone on and on about what a brilliant detective he was and how she'd remembered his

derhill sneered, somewhat taken aback that the cowed pup had the nerve to fight back, even a little.

"Perhaps he won't believe me, but the police will." Grant appeared to gain courage as he spoke. "It's not the first time you've done it. I know that much."

Underhill watched him for a moment, his expression amused. "What you know is one thing. What you can prove is something else entirely. You weren't complaining when you got your money, little man. I suspect the police will be interested in that too."

Grant's bravado deserted him completely. He lifted his hand and ran it nervously through his thin, blond hair. "Look, let's not get silly over this. It's in both our interests to cooperate with each other."

Underhill's lip curled in derision. "You really are a cowardly little whelp, aren't you? Well, lucky for you I happen to need money. Otherwise, you'd be on your own. We made a deal and I kept my part of it. So if you want my help now, I suggest you keep your mouth shut and do precisely as I say."

"Arthur." Mary Grant's voice interrupted their conversation.

The two men turned and saw the elegant middle-aged woman with graying blond hair and cool blue eyes standing in the doorway of the drawing room. "We do have guests, Arthur," she said. "Would you and Mr. Underhill like to join us now or will you be having your tea in the hall?"

Arthur gulped. "We'll be right there, Mama."

She nodded regally and turned away. Underhill snickered. "You're more scared of her than you are of him."

Arthur would have dearly liked to deny it, but he couldn't. He was frightened of his father. But he was positively terrified of his stepmother. "We'd better go in. She hates to be kept waiting."

Underhill laughed aloud. He was going to enjoy annoying Mary Grant today. He owed her that much for the way she'd helped humiliate him earlier. But perhaps the pup was right; perhaps he oughtn't annoy the lady too much. Not just yet, anyway.

Together, the two men went into the drawing room just as a maid came up the hall pushing an elaborate tea trolley.

"Girl," Underhill said to the maid, "go out in the garden and see if my mints are there. I think I left them on the table. They're in a red-and-white tin."

"Yes, sir," the maid answered. She placed the trolley carefully in front of where Mary Grant was sitting and scurried off.

"Will your husband be joining us for tea, Mrs. Grant?" Tyrell Modean asked.

"Of course. He only went into his study for a moment. I believe he's gone to get *The Times*. I think there's a notice he'd like you to see. There are some old tapestry panels being offered for sale. Neville thought you might be interested in acquiring them for your museum." She smiled warmly at the handsome American. Her smile slipped a bit when she glanced at Modean's wife.

Lydia Modean was too beautiful to be liked and too rich to be ignored, despite the fact that she'd once made her living posing for half the artists in Soho.

A thumping came from down the hallway and Mary steeled herself to continue being gracious as her husband, deliberately slamming his cane against the floor, banged into the room.

His thinning white hair was disheveled, his watery eyes glittering with rage. "Call the police," he thundered. "Someone's stolen my paintings. My Caldararos. They're gone!"

kindness and sensitivity from that awful Slocum murder. Then she'd started to cry and — well, to be honest, he'd have agreed to anything to get her to stop. So here he was, trotting along to some man's house and preparing to ask a few uncomfortable questions. He hoped this Mr. Grant would be civil about it. Witherspoon brushed his doubts aside. Surely he wasn't stepping out of line merely by making a few inquiries. After all, he was a police officer and a young woman had gone missing.

"Miss Lanier was certain of the address, sir," Smythe replied. He hoped they'd done the right thing in having Nanette throw herself upon the inspector's good nature. Cor blimey, he'd hate to see the inspector get the sticky end of the wicket over this, especially as it was really their problem, not his.

But none of the household had been able to resist, as Mrs. Jeffries had put it, "putting the cat amongst the pigeons." If nothing else, it would get the servants at the Grant house gossiping and speculating. Always a handy situation when it came to solving cases, Smythe reckoned. "Number thirty-four, Beltrane Gardens. It's just up there, sir," he said.

Witherspoon stiffened his spine and charged ahead. Best to get this over with.

"No one's stolen anything, Neville," Mary said calmly. She smoothed the folds of her elegant brown tea gown. "Arthur suggested I send the

Caldararos out to be cleaned before Mr. Modean's expert has a look at them."

"Who told you to do that?" Grant grumbled, more out of habit than anger. Mary, for all her shortcomings as a woman, was a jolly fine household manager. The paintings had become a bit scruffy. He was just surprised that his half wit of a son had the foresight to suggest it.

Mary was unperturbed. "The frames were getting quite dirty. Now do sit down and have tea. Cook has surpassed herself this afternoon." She surveyed the loaded trolley with a critical eye. There were two kinds of sandwiches, tongue and ham. Tea, of course, in the silver-plated pot as well as a smaller silver pot of coffee. A plate of balmorals sat beside a tray of fancy biscuits. Next to that was an urn of heavy cream, a perfect madeira cake and a Victorian sponge. She nodded, satisfied that her kitchen wouldn't shame her in front of her guests.

"Everything certainly looks lovely," Lydia Modean said quickly. She glanced at the others in the room. Nobody looked like they were having a very nice time.

Arthur Grant was perched on the edge of a chair, his fingers nervously scratching the silk lapels of his elegant gray frock coat. Neville Grant, dressed less formally in a black morning coat and wing-tipped collar, had thumped over and flopped down on the settee. Mary Grant was sitting behind the tea cart, her mouth curved in a slight smile, her eyes glittering coldly.

Lydia avoided looking at Underhill. Watching the man smirk at her when they'd been outside had been bad enough.

"Have you enjoyed your visit?" Arthur Grant asked timidly.

"Very much," Tyrell replied graciously, though he'd already answered that same query out in the garden. "London is a beautiful city." He patted his wife's hand. "I do believe that Johnson was correct when he wrote, 'When a man is tired of London, he is tired of life, for there is in London all that life can afford.' "

"You've read Samuel Johnson?" Underhill inquired archly. "How fascinating. I hadn't realized one could acquire a classical education in your part of the world."

Refusing to rise to the bait, Tyrell merely shrugged. "San Francisco has many fine educational establishments. Unfortunately, I never had the opportunity to acquire much formal education. I'm basically self-educated. Like so many *successful*" — he stressed the last word ever so slightly — "men of my country, I relied upon myself, not my family, to make my way in the world."

Underhill flushed angrily as the barb struck home. Everyone in the room knew he'd dissipated the fortune his family had left him. A series of disastrous investments had forced him to sell the once extensive Underhill art collection as well as the family estate. The only thing left was a small cottage out in some unfashionable part of the countryside. Underhill now made a living using the only skill he had. An eye for art. He hung about the fringes of the art world, brokering deals and acting as an art agent.

"And you, Mrs. Modean?" Arthur inquired hastily. "Are you enjoying your visit?"

"Yes," she replied. "But I'm anxious to go home."

"You don't miss England, then?" Underhill asked. "I should think you'd miss your old friends."

"My wife loves San Francisco," Tyrell interjected smoothly.

Underhill ignored Modean and kept his attention fully on Mrs. Modean. "But surely you must miss the cultural aspects of our great city. I believe you were once quite involved with the art world yourself."

Lydia stared at him for a moment, debating on whether or not to be openly rude. "I was an artists' model," she replied calmly, giving her husband a quick look. He gave her a warm smile. "And to be perfectly honest, I'm afraid I'm not as enamored of London as Tyrell. I prefer the 'cultural aspects' of San Francisco. Last Saturday we went to a sale of supposed 'Old Masters' at Christie's. There wasn't anything worth mentioning in the whole lot."

"I don't know, my dear," her husband said, his eyes sparkling with amusement. "I would have liked to have had that Morland."

"Why?" Lydia countered bluntly. "You didn't like it."

"No," he agreed, "but Morland's work has continued to rise in value and it would have made a nice addition to the collection for the museum. Too bad that other fellow got his hands on it."

"Did it sell for a lot of money?" Arthur asked.

Tyrell shook his head. "Not really. A few hundred pounds."

"Three hundred and thirty-six pounds," Underhill muttered. He knew precisely what everything in that collection had sold for. He'd been there. "If it wasn't much money, why didn't you buy it?"

"I didn't want it that badly," Tyrell answered, looking him straight in the eye, "and the other fellow did."

"So your trip here is business more than pleasure," Mary said conversationally.

"As you've probably guessed, it's a bit of both." Tyrell patted Lydia's arm. "Lydia does have some old friends and relations she likes to stay in touch with. But basically we're here to acquire for the museum. That reminds me. I got a cable from the other board members. They're delighted your husband has agreed to sell the Caldararos."

"I understand the paintings were originally from your family's collection?" Lydia said.

Mary nodded. "They'd been in my family for over two hundred years when I married Neville." She reached for the teapot. "How do you take your tea, Mrs. Modean?"

"Plain, please," Lydia replied.

"When will the paintings be ready?" Tyrell asked.

The maid came back holding a small red-and-white tin. She skirted around the group of guests and handed them to Underhill. "Your tin of mints, sir," she whispered, giving him a quick curtsy and then hurrying out.

Underhill gave the tin a small shake, flipped the lid open and frowned. Two left. Bloody girl. She'd no doubt helped herself. He'd make a fuss but he didn't want to give that wretched American an excuse for thinking him ill-mannered. He'd show them what good breeding was, by God. He popped the last two in his mouth and slapped the lid down.

"In a few days," Mary replied. "Why? Are you in a hurry for them? I understood you weren't leaving until the end of next week."

"It's not that we're in a rush, Mrs. Grant," he explained. "It's that Mr. Marceau, the expert we've hired to authenticate the paintings, is going to Paris on Monday next. I'd hoped to have everything concluded by then."

"Oh, I'm dreadfully sorry. I didn't mean to be so late." This comment was uttered by Helen Collier, Mary Grant's sister. Her face was long and bony, her hair a light brown and worn in a girlish style. Frizzed at the front and plaited low on the neck in a rolled braid, the coiffure was not suited to one of her middle years. She hurried into the drawing room, an apologetic smile on her thin lips. "Do forgive me."

"How's your headache?" Mary asked. "Any better?"

"Much. Thank you for asking." Helen smiled coquettishly at Underhill as she took the chair next to him. He gave her a nod in return and raised his hand to cover his mouth as he coughed.

"It's amazing what having even a little lay down can do for one," she said airily.

"I'm glad you're feeling better," Tyrell said gallantly. He thought females who developed sick headaches from a few minutes in the miserably weak English sun were poor excuses for women. "We were just having the most interesting discussion about English art."

Underhill's coughing got louder, but everyone politely ignored it.

"I'm so sorry to have missed it," Helen said enthusiastically. "Art is one of my great loves."

A peculiar, strangling gasp suddenly filled the quiet room. It took a moment or two before anyone realized the strange sound was actually coming from Underhill. He gasped again and then again before opening his mouth completely, as if he were going to scream. But only great, choking, wheezing croaks were emitted from his thin throat.

Modean was the first to realize something was seriously wrong. He leapt to his feet and dashed to the stricken man. "Good God, what's wrong with you, man?"

Underhill's eyes bulged and his pale skin flushed as he struggled to drag air into his chest.

"He must be choking on those damned mints," Modean cried, lifting his hand and slapping the man's back.

But it didn't help. Underhill began thrashing about on the cushions, his hands clawing at the tight collar of his white silk shirt.

Helen screamed. "Oh, God. Someone do something."

By this time everyone, even Neville Grant, had moved toward the man flailing about on the settee. Underhill slipped off his seat and landed on the carpet with a thud, his legs kicking so wildly he clipped Helen on the arm. She screamed again and Lydia Modean pulled her back out of the way.

"Give them some space," Lydia ordered.

Tyrell wrestled Underhill onto his back and yanked off the tight buttons of his collar, freeing his throat. But that made no difference. His face turned white, so white it was almost bluish in color.

"For God's sake, what's wrong with him?" Mary demanded. "Is he having a fit?"

Suddenly the thrashing stopped.

James Underhill went completely still.

Modean bent down and put his ear to the man's chest. He raised his hand for silence as he listened. For a moment the room was quiet. But then Modean straightened and looked up at the others. He shook his head.

"Well, what's wrong with the fellow?" Neville Grant asked brusquely. "Is he sick? Should we call a doctor?"

"That's not going to do him any good now," Modean replied as he rose to his feet. "He's dead. I think you'd better call the police."

"Dead?" Neville poked at the lifeless form with his cane. "Are you sure?"

"For God's sake, Neville, stop that," Mary snapped.

"Dead? But that's impossible," Helen Collier wailed.

Lydia Modean closed her eyes.

Arthur Grant slumped into the nearest chair.

Mary Grant stiffened her spine, strode to the bell pull and gave it a hard tug. Almost immediately the doors opened and the butler appeared. His gaze swept the room, his eyes widening as he espied Underhill lying in front of the settee.

Before any of the Grants could issue an order, Tyrell Modean spoke. "Send for the police," he instructed the surprised servant. "We've a dead man here."

"That won't be necessary, sir." The butler swallowed nervously. "They're already here."

"The police? Here?" Neville Grant stomped past the butler and into the hallway. Standing by the front door, he spotted three men. "Don't just stand there," he called. "Come on. It's in here."

Witherspoon stared at the apparition at the opposite end of the hall. The gentleman seemed to be talking to them.

"I say," he murmured to Smythe. "This looks like it might be a tad easier than I thought. The fellow certainly seems eager to answer questions."

"Do get a move on," the elderly man shouted, waving at them impatiently with his cane. "Why aren't you in uniform? You'd better be the police or I'll have your . . ."

"I am a policeman," Witherspoon assured him, "and these gentlemen" — he gestured at Smythe and Wiggins — "are from my household. Now, if you don't mind, I'd like to ask you a few questions."

"For God's sake, Neville," Mary shouted from the open door of the drawing room. "Bring them here."

"This way, this way." Grant turned on his heel and started back the way he'd just come.

"Cor blimey," the coachman muttered, "what's goin' on 'ere?"

"I don't know," Witherspoon replied honestly. "But I do believe he wants us to follow him." He hurried after the man, and after a moment's hesitation, Wiggins and Smythe trotted after him.

Witherspoon stopped short when he entered the drawing room. A group of elegantly dressed people stood staring down at a man lying on the carpet. The inspector, thinking the man was injured, flew across the room and dropped to his knees. "What's happened here?"

"We've no idea," a woman replied archly.

Witherspoon felt for a pulse. There was none.

44

But that didn't mean the fellow was gone. He looked at Wiggins. "Run and fetch the constable on the corner. Tell him to find a doctor and get here right away."

"That won't do any good," a man with an American accent said. "He's dead."

"How long?"

"A few moments ago," the American continued. "He choked to death. He was eating those hard confectionaries. Mints, I think. They must have lodged in his throat."

"Fetch a doctor anyway," Witherspoon ordered Wiggins. "It might not be too late." The footman took off at a run.

"Poor bloke," Smythe muttered. He dropped down next to the inspector. "What 'appened?"

"We just told you. He choked to death," Mary Grant replied. "We were sitting here having tea when all of a sudden, he started gasping for air and then he simply keeled over."

"Oh, no," Helen wailed. "He can't be gone, he simply can't."

Mary ignored her sister and kept her gaze on the two men kneeling by Underhill. One of them looked like a brutal street thug and the other, though far more respectably dressed, looked like a bank clerk. "You say you're from the police?"

Witherspoon nodded slowly but didn't look up. "I'm Inspector Gerald Witherspoon."

Helen continued to sob. As no one else in the room took any notice of the woman, Lydia Modean put an arm around her and led her away. "I'll just take her up to her room," she murmured to her husband.

"What should we do now, sir?" Smythe asked the inspector.

Witherspoon wasn't sure. There was something decidedly odd about this situation. He swallowed hard and forced himself to continue examining the body. The inspector was a bit squeamish about corpses. Then he wondered if this one could really count as a corpse. After all, the poor man had only just died a few moments ago.

"What was his name?" he asked. He had the strangest feeling the man hadn't choked to death. For one thing, the fellow's mouth was gaping open and he could see two small, round, white objects stuck to the roof of his mouth.

"James Underhill," a male voice replied.

Smythe cleared his throat. "Uh, sir . . ."

"Oh, sorry, Smythe." He looked up and gave his coachman a weary smile. Then he looked at the imposing woman standing over him. "Madam, would you be so kind as to take everyone to another room? I'd like to have a few moments of privacy to examine this gentleman."

"We'll go into the morning room," she said. "It's just down the hall."

Smythe waited till they were alone and then said, "Is something wrong, sir?"

"I don't think this fellow choked to death, Smythe," Witherspoon said. He took a deep breath, forced the man's jaws further open and stuck his hand into the dead man's mouth.

"What are you doin', sir?" Smythe hissed, shocked to his very core.

Witherspoon jerked his fingers out and exhaled the breath he'd been holding. "Checking to see if there was any obstruction in his throat." He gasped. "There isn't. Would you please reach into my coat pocket and grab my handkerchief?" His hands were covered with spittle and he didn't want to get it on his clothing.

Perplexed, the coachman did as instructed and pulled a clean, white cotton hankie out of the inspector's inside pocket.

"Could you open it, please," Witherspoon directed, "and hold it firmly on the sides?" He took another deep breath and stuck his fingers between the corpse's lips.

Smythe spread the material as instructed. He felt his stomach contract as the inspector slowly eased his hand out — and there on the tip of his finger was a small, round, white object.

"He couldn't choke on this if he'd not swallowed it," Witherspoon murmured, carefully depositing the object in the center of the outspread handkerchief.

Smythe still couldn't believe what he'd just seen. "Shouldn't we wait for the doctor before we go pokin' at the poor feller?"

"Normally, yes." Witherspoon hoped he wouldn't faint. "But in this case, I want to make sure our evidence doesn't melt."

"Cor blimey, sir." Smythe shook his head as he

saw the inspector repeating what he'd just done. "You've a stronger stomach than I do."

"No, I don't." Witherspoon hoped he'd keep his dinner down. "I assure you, this is quite the most difficult thing I've done in a very long time." It was his duty that forced him to do such an abominable thing. But duty was duty and despite his revulsion, he had to know the truth. "Despite what the witnesses said, I've an idea this man didn't choke to death."

Smythe's heavy brows creased. "What are ya thinkin', sir?"

"Well . . ." The inspector didn't wish to "jump the gun," so to speak. But his "inner voice," that instinct that Mrs. Jeffries was always reminding him to listen to, was prompting him along a certain course of action. "I'm thinking he couldn't have choked if the confectionaries were on the roof of his mouth and not obstructing a breathing passage. Furthermore, he's a young man, probably not past his thirtieth year. His limbs appear to be straight." The inspector examined the man's hands. "His skin isn't discolored and there's no sign of blood or any other injury. Except for being dead, he looks to be in relatively good health. He's not particularly fat or diseased looking . . ." He paused, not quite sure to put what he was thinking into words.

"Right, sir," the coachman agreed. "Except for him bein' dead and all, he looks right healthy to me too."

"So it seems to me if he keeled over in the

middle of tea, he might have been" — he hesitated — "poisoned."

"He's been poisoned." Dr. Bosworth rose to his feet and nodded at the constable. "Go ahead and take him away," he instructed. "I'll do the full postmortem at the hospital."

"Are you certain?" Witherspoon pressed.

"As sure as I can be without doing an autopsy," Bosworth replied. He was a tall man with a thin, serious face and red hair. "But if I were a betting man, I'd say that poor fellow had ingested potassium cyanide."

"What, precisely, makes you think so?" Witherspoon wanted to be as certain as possible before he started asking questions.

Bosworth hesitated only briefly. "There's a faint scent of bitter almond on the man's lips. From the color of his skin, I'd say he died of asphyxiation. As no one admits to choking the life out of the poor fellow, I'd wager he must have ingested something to cause such a reaction."

"Could it have been on one of these?" Witherspoon opened the handkerchief he'd been holding and held it out so the doctor could see it clearly. "Mints, I believe. I took them out of the victim's mouth."

"May I?" Bosworth asked. He brought the open handkerchief close to his face. His face was a mask of concentration as he took a long, deep breath. "Hum . . . yes, unless I'm very much mistaken, underneath the mint scent is bitter almonds." He looked at the inspector. "Have you touched these?"

"Only with the tip of my finger."

"Then you'd best go wash your hands soon. Ask one of the servants to show you to a cloak-room and be sure to use plenty of soap." Bosworth waved the constables carrying a stretcher into the room.

While the inspector hurried off to wash up and the doctor supervised getting the body moved, Smythe took a few moments to suss out the lay of the house. He tiptoed out into the hallway and peeked into a room a little further up the hall. They were all in there. The old gent with the cane was stomping about muttering something under his breath. The American was sitting next to his wife, his arm draped around her shoulders. The other two women were standing next to the window. The one with the frizzy brown hair had stopped crying and was talking in a low, hissing whisper. Smythe thought she looked mad enough to spit nails. The tall, regal-looking one didn't seem to be paying any attention to her. She just stood there, tapping her foot and shooting glares at the pale-faced young man. He sat on the chair, looking like he'd just lost his best friend.

"Oh, there you are, Smythe." The inspector appeared from around the corner.

"What are you goin' to do, sir?" Smythe was itching to get back and tell the others, but at the same time, he was loathe to leave the inspector.

He didn't want to miss anything.

"I'm not sure, Smythe," Witherspoon admitted. "Officially, this isn't a murder investigation yet, only a death under suspicious circumstances. I'm not certain I ought to do anything except trot along to the station and make a report."

"But if it is a murder," the coachman pressed, "probably one of them" — he jerked his head toward the room the others were in — "had something to do with it. If you let 'em loose without questionin' 'em, they might muck up or destroy any evidence that's 'ere."

"I know."

"You can at least question 'em, sir," Smythe persisted. "Like ya said, it is a death under suspicious circumstances."

"Of course it is," Witherspoon decided. Turning, he called to the constable standing beside the open front door. "Constable, send to the police station and inform the duty sergeant that there's been a suspicious death at this house. After that I'd like you to fetch Constable Barnes. He's off duty, but you can get his address."

"I'm already here, sir." A tall man with a craggy face stepped through the front door. "Wiggins fetched me, sir. He thought you might need me."

"I 'ope I did right, sir," Wiggins said cautiously.

"Yes, Wiggins, you did."

"What've we got, sir?" Barnes asked as he advanced toward his superior.

"A suspicious death," Witherspoon replied. "Luckily, Dr. Bosworth happened to be available." He stepped back to let the constables carrying the stretcher move past him towards the front door.

"There was nothing lucky about it," Bosworth commented as he stepped into the hall. "I was on my way to see you, Inspector. I'd just gotten off the omnibus on the Holland Park Road when your lad came dashing up to the constable. He spotted me and told me there was a possible death here." Dr. Bosworth wasn't telling the whole truth. As a matter of fact, he'd been on his way to the inspector's house, but it was Mrs. Jeffries he'd wanted to visit, not the inspector. But as his association with Mrs. Jeffries generally involved one of the inspector's cases, and as he was now part of the conspiracy of silence surrounding the household's help in those cases, he was in a bit of a quandry.

"You were on your way to see me?" Witherspoon said, somewhat perplexed.

"I wanted to invite you to dine with me one evening next week," Bosworth replied. "A colleague of mine from New York is in London. I thought you might be interested in meeting him. He works very closely with the New York police. Like myself, he's a doctor." The invitation was quite genuine. But Bosworth had meant it for Mrs. Jeffries. She was someone whose abilities rather astonished him.

"Oh." Witherspoon was quite flattered. "How very kind of you, Dr. Bosworth. I'd like that very much."

Bosworth smiled absently and started toward the door.

"Excuse me, sir." One of the constables came out of the drawing room. "I've found this, sir." He hesitated, not knowing whether to give the object in his hand to the doctor or the inspector. "It's a tin of peppermints. I saw it under the settee when we moved the body."

Witherspoon nodded for the constable to relinquish the tin to Bosworth, who took it and flipped open the lid. Holding it to his nose, he sniffed. "Ah ha." He shoved the tin under Witherspoon's nose. "Can you smell it?"

Witherspoon took a deep breath. Even though the tin was empty and all he was smelling was the inside paper wrapper, the scent was unmistakable. Faint, perhaps, but definitely there despite being masked by the overpowering mint scent. "Almonds," he said, raising his eyes to meet the doctor's. "Bitter almonds. Do you think it's cyanide?" He didn't want to make any rash accusations. But he didn't wish to ignore evidence either.

"Probably," Bosworth replied. "I'll run an analysis. Unfortunately, there aren't any mints left, only the paper, the half-eaten mints and a few grains of residue powder. Still, there should be enough to give us a definite answer one way or another."

"By all means, Doctor," Witherspoon agreed quickly. "Run the tests. Be sure and mark it into evidence with the constables."

"I know the procedure, Inspector." Bosworth grinned cheerfully. "Even if I'm not on my own patch tonight. Well, I'd best be going. I'll get started on the PM early tomorrow morning. We ought to know something definite straight away."

"You'll not have any difficulty with the local police surgeon, will you?" Witherspoon asked. Bosworth's comment had made him realize this whole procedure was highly irregular. The post-mortem was supposed to be done by the local doctor assigned to this district.

Bosworth shook his head. "I'm assigned to Westminster, Inspector. So I'm having the body taken to St. Thomas's. There shouldn't be any difficulty. The local doctor for this district is a colleague of mine and a friend. He'll not make a fuss. He's enough on his plate as it is." He nodded goodbye and left.

"What do we do now, sir?" Barnes asked.

"I'd best send Smythe and Wiggins home," Witherspoon muttered. But when he turned around, neither one of them was anywhere to be found.

"I knew that once Constable Barnes arrived, we'd not 'ave much of an excuse to keep 'angin' about," Smythe explained. "So I 'ot footed it back 'ere to let you know what was goin' on so we could get crackin' on it."

Smythe and Wiggins had told the household everything that occurred since they'd left the house with the inspector in tow.

"Are we sure it's a murder, then?" Betsy asked suspiciously. She didn't want to get her hopes up and then find out the man had dropped dead from something else.

"We won't know for sure until tomorrow," Smythe replied, "but Dr. Bosworth seemed to think it was poison."

Mrs. Jeffries had a dozen different questions to ask, but right now, she didn't have the time. If this was a case of deliberate poisoning, then the sooner they got started, the better. "I think we ought to proceed on the assumption that it is murder. Did you manage to find out the names of the people present at the Grant house?" she asked hopefully, looking at Smythe.

"I didn't 'ave time," he admitted.

"I did," Wiggins volunteered.

Smythe slanted him a suspicious glance. " 'Ow'd you manage that with all yer toin' and froin'?"

"I'm fast when I want to be," he said proudly. "And I nipped down to the kitchen after I brung the constable. Two of the 'ousemaids was nat-terin' on about what 'ad 'appened. They named names, if ya know what I mean. Seems the fellow who died was named Underhill. The woman doin' all the screamin' when we come in was Helen Collier. She's sister to Mr. Neville Grant's wife, Mary. She was glarin' like a tartar and actin' like the bloke dyin' was a personal insult. Neville Grant was an old bloke with a cane and there was a pale-faced feller that looked like he'd just lost his best friend — that was Arthur Grant, Neville's son. The two others were an American couple by the name of Modean."

Awed, they all stared at him. Wiggins shrugged. "The 'ousemaids was natterin' like a couple of magpies. I'da 'eard more but that stick of a butler come by and chased 'em both about their business."

"So at least we've a few names to start with," Mrs. Goodge said triumphantly.

"We'd best send for Luty and Hatchet," Betsy said. "You know how they get when we don't send for them right away."

Smythe looked at Mrs. Jeffries. "Should I go?"

"The inspector might take it upon himself to start asking questions tonight," she said thoughtfully. "On the other hand, he might come home quite soon."

"I think Smythe ought to go straight away," Mrs. Goodge said stoutly. "The worst that can happen is the inspector comin' in and finding them here. But he'd think nothing of it. They're good friends."

"Go ahead, Smythe," Mrs. Jeffries instructed. "See if you can get them here quickly. We've much to discuss."

As soon as Smythe had disappeared, she turned to Wiggins. "Was there any sign of Irene Simmons at the Grant house?"

Wiggins shook his head. "Nothin'. That's one of the reasons I nipped down to the kitchen. I wanted to 'ave a bit of a look about the place. But I didn't see anything."

"Do you think this man dyin' and Irene Simmons might be connected?" Betsy asked.

Mrs. Jeffries wasn't sure. "I don't know. It would be so much simpler if we knew for certain this man was murdered."

"For the sake of argument, let's say he was," Mrs. Goodge suggested.

"Then I'd say the disappearance of Irene Simmons is connected in some way with the dead man," she replied.

"Good." Mrs. Goodge lit the fire on the stove. "That'll make it nice and simple-like. I'll just put some water on to boil. We might as well have tea when Luty and Hatchet get here. It'll help us keep our wits about us."

"I'll get the cups," Betsy volunteered.

They kept themselves busy tidying up and setting the table. Finally, after what seemed like hours, they heard the sound of a carriage pulling up outside.

"They're here," Mrs. Jeffries said as she took her seat at the head of the table.

"Land o' Goshen," Luty cried, "thank goodness Smythe got there when he did. We was fixin' to go out."

She was an elderly American woman with sharp black eyes, white hair and a penchant for bright clothes. Her small frame was swathed in a deep crimson evening jacket decorated with ostrich feathers. Tossing her handbag onto the table, she snatched out the chair next to the housekeeper and flopped down.

"Good evening, everyone," Hatchet, her tall, white-haired, dignified butler said as he followed his mistress into the kitchen. He was dressed as always: pristine white shirt, black frock coat and trousers. "It is rather fortunate that Smythe arrived when he did. We were about to leave for Lord Staunton's dinner party." He tossed a malevolent glance at Luty. "Unfortunately, Madam didn't have time to send her regrets to Lord Staunton."

"Piddle." Luty waved a hand dismissively. "That old windbag has so many people cluttering up his place he'll not notice if I'm there or not. I ain't missin' me a murder to go have supper with a bunch of people I don't even like. I would'na accepted the invitation in the first place if you hadn't nagged me into it."

The American woman was rich, eccentric and had a heart as big as the country that had spawned her. Her butler was smart, devoted to his mistress and a bit of a martinet. They were dear friends of the household, having worked with them on a number of the inspector's cases.

Hatchet raised one eyebrow and drew out a chair for himself. "I never nag, madam. However, like you, I didn't want to risk missing out either."

"We ready, then?" Smythe asked, dropping

into the chair next to Betsy.

"Yes," Mrs. Jeffries replied. "If no one objects, I'll start." She told the newcomers everything, beginning with Nanette Lanier's unexpected visit. "So you see," she finished, "we may have called you out under false pretenses. We don't know that we do have a murder here. Underhill might have died from natural causes."

"If he did, then I'm the Queen of Sheba," Luty declared. "A disappearin' woman and a dead man in the same house within days of each other." She snorted. "Somethin' funny's goin' on, that's for sure."

"I quite agree," Hatchet added. "One extraordinary event might be explainable, but two? No, Mrs. Jeffries, you were right to send for us. Something strange is indeed going on in that household."

"So what do we do now?" Mrs. Goodge asked. She glanced anxiously in the direction of her larders. Her provisions were low and she had to do a bit of baking to feed her sources. People loosened their tongues better over a slice of cake or a good currant bun.

"Well," Mrs. Jeffries said slowly, "I think we ought to proceed as we usually do. Though there is something we must keep in mind."

"What's that?" Wiggins asked, picking up his mug and taking a sip.

"We did promise Nanette we'd find her friend."

"But you said they was probably connected," Smythe declared.

"Might be connected," she corrected. "Then again, one thing may have nothing to do with the other. We did make a promise. We must honor our word."

"Does that mean we can't get crackin' on this 'ere murder?" Wiggins asked the question that all of them were thinking.

"It means," Mrs. Jeffries said firmly, "that we might have to do both."

Chapter 3

"We'd best take statements tonight," Inspector Witherspoon said to Barnes. "I think we'd better have a quick word with the members of the household."

"Right, sir," Barnes agreed. He stifled a yawn and cast a longing glance at the loaded tea trolley. Tea would be nice right about now. Then he remembered the victim might have been poisoned and suddenly he wasn't quite so thirsty. "Do you want to speak to everyone together or should I bring them in one at a time?"

"One at a time, I think," Witherspoon said. "This is, after all, a suspicious death. Start with the elderly gentleman. We might as well hear what he's got to say so he can get to bed. People that age need their rest. Have the police constables take statements from the servants."

"Yes, sir," Barnes said, moving smartly toward the door. As soon as he'd disappeared, the inspector took a few moments to study his surroundings. No shortage of money here, he thought, as his gaze flicked about the huge room.

An elegant crystal chandelier, ablaze with

light, cast a bright glow over the exquisite furnishings. Oil paintings in ornate gold frames and
family portraits were beautifully set off by the
pale, wheat-colored walls. Dark panelling, its
wood shining in the reflected glow of the chan-
deliers, covered the lower half of the walls. The
furnishings were as elegant as the house itself:
settees in heavy blue and gold damask, two
groupings of high-backed upholstered velveteen
chairs and tables covered with silk-fringed
shawls. Heavy royal-blue curtains were draped
artistically across the windows.

His gaze came to rest on the tea trolley. He
wondered if he ought to take it into evidence.

"What's all this nonsense, then?"

Witherspoon whirled about just as Barnes and
the elderly gentleman entered the drawing room.
"What's the matter?" the man snapped at the inspector. "Cat got your tongue? Why are you still
here and why does this person" — he pointed his
cane at Barnes — "insist I make a statement like
I'm some kind of a criminal? Underhill choked
on one of those wretched mints he was always
popping in his mouth. That's all I've got to say
on the subject."

"And you are?" Witherspoon asked politely.

"Neville Grant. I own this house."

"I'm sorry to inconvenience you, Mr. Grant,"
the inspector said apologetically, "but there is
some question as to how Mr. Underhill met his
death."

"What do you mean?" Grant sputtered.

"There's no question as to how he died. He choked to death. I saw it with my own eyes."

"Then you'll make an excellent witness, sir," Witherspoon assured him. "Now, I suggest we all sit down. Constable, will you be so kind as to take notes?"

"That'll not be so 'ard," Wiggins said cheerfully. "We can keep a lookout for Miss Lanier's friend while we're sussin' out who killed this Underhill bloke."

"Seems to me if the two things are connected," Betsy added thoughtfully, "we shouldn't have any problems getting information about Irene Simmons while we're digging for clues on the murder."

"Should be dead easy," Smythe agreed.

"Could be the girl's run off with some artist," Luty put in. "Could be she ain't missin' at all."

Mrs. Jeffries was afraid she wasn't making her point. "It could be that the two events aren't at all linked," she said firmly, "and it might be quite difficult to do both investigations at once. I must remind you, we did agree to help Nanette find her friend."

A heavy, guilty quiet descended on the kitchen. Everyone tried to pretend they didn't really understand what Mrs. Jeffries was trying to tell them. Finally, Smythe cleared his throat. "What are ya tryin' to tell us?"

"I'm simply trying to point out that we have a prior obligation."

"You want us to find out who snatched Miss Simmons before we can start trackin' Underhill's killer?" Wiggins asked incredulously.

"I didn't say that," Mrs. Jeffries objected. "But it may be necessary for us to divide our resources. Some of us might need to work on the Underhill matter and some of us might need to investigate Miss Simmons's disappearance. There's no reason we can't do both at the same time. There are" — she swept her arm out in an arc, a gesture that encompassed the entire group — "rather a lot of us. We can easily handle both tasks."

Again, no one said anything. The silence spoke volumes about what they were thinking. The mystery surrounding Irene Simmons's disappearance was definitely second fiddle to a possible murder case. Everyone wanted to investigate the murder. But no one wanted to be the first to admit it.

Hatchet broke the impasse. "I'll be quite happy to lend my efforts to locating the girl," he volunteered. "After all, Underhill is already dead. This young woman may still be alive."

"I'll help find Irene too," Betsy added. Her conscience had gotten the best of her as well. "I mean, I like investigatin' murder and all, but Hatchet's right. Irene Simmons might be alive and needing help."

Satisfied, Mrs. Jeffries smiled. She'd been fairly sure they'd do what was right. If need be, she'd been quite prepared to take on the task of locating Irene Simmons herself. "Excellent. I, of course, shall be assisting in both matters. Now, let's see what we can come up with for tomorrow. Betsy, why don't you use your resources to find out if anyone in the Grant household knew the girl."

"All right," Betsy replied brightly. While she was at it, she'd suss out a few things about this murder too. "I'll have a go at the local shopkeepers tomorrow as well. Perhaps one of them saw Irene."

"There ain't no shops on Beltrane Gardens," Wiggins told her, trying to be helpful.

Betsy shot him a frown. "Well, someone might have seen her walking on Holland Park Road. There's shops along there. Just because Nanette claims the girl never came out of the Grant house, that doesn't make it a fact. Someone might have seen her and we won't know for certain unless we ask."

"You're right, Betsy," Mrs. Jeffries interjected. "As we've learned from our past cases, we mustn't take everything we're told at face value. Nanette Lanier could easily be mistaken about the real facts surrounding Irene's disappearance." She knew good and well that Betsy wasn't one to let a chance pass her by. The maid would do her utmost to find the missing girl, but while she was at it, Mrs. Jeffries knew she'd get as much information as possible about the Grant household and James Underhill.

"As I shall be using my rather considerable resources to locate the girl," Hatchet declared, "and Miss Betsy will be using her own exceptional detecting and observation skills, I'm sure we'll have the young woman home safe and sound in no time." He beamed encouragingly at the maid, who smiled in return.

"What do ya mean, 'resources'?" Luty demanded suspiciously. It galled her that her own butler constantly got the jump on her when it came to hunting down clues. The man had more sources to tap for information in this city than a dog had fleas. She wasn't fooled for one minute by his pronouncement, either. She knew good and well he'd be snooping about looking for Underhill's killer at the same time he was trying to find the Simmons girl.

Hatchet allowed himself a small smirk. "I believe, madam, we agreed on a previous occasion that some of our resources were to be kept secret. Even from one another. If you don't mind, I'd rather not say what or who I'll be using in my investigations."

"Use whatever means you have at your disposal," Mrs. Jeffries said quickly. Luty and Hatchet, despite their devotion to one another, were fierce competitors when it came to investigations. "And the rest of you, please, don't feel that because Betsy and Hatchet are taking the primary responsibility for locating Miss Simmons that the rest of you won't be expected to do your fair share. All of us must do our best to find her."

"Of course we will," Mrs. Goodge agreed stoutly. Mentally, she made a list of people she could drag into her kitchen tomorrow. It wouldn't hurt to ask a few questions about missing models while she was at it.

Hatchet leaned forward on one elbow. "Before I forget, Mrs. Jeffries, would you please give me a brief description of Miss Simmons?"

Mrs. Jeffries cringed, disgusted at herself for overlooking such an important detail. "Oh my goodness, I never thought to ask Nanette Lanier. Gracious, how silly of me."

"None of us thought of it, either," Smythe said, seeing the housekeeper's stricken expression. "Don't be so 'ard on yerself. Guess we was all so excited about gettin' somethin' to do, we forgot one of the most important bits. Findin' out what she looked like." He shook his head in disbelief.

"I know what she's like," Wiggins announced cheerfully. "She's got dark brown hair, green eyes and she's about my height."

"Cor blimey, 'ow'd you know that?" Smythe demanded.

"I asked Miss Lanier when I walked 'er out to get a 'ansom," he explained. "She told me Miss Simmons was wearing one of her old dresses too. It were a dark blue wool with white piping on the jacket."

"Excellent, Wiggins," Mrs. Jeffries congratulated him.

"I thought it might be important," he replied modestly.

"And it is important." Hatchet clapped the footman on the back. "Well done, lad. Well done. Armed with that pertinent information, Miss Betsy and I will really be able to get cracking on finding our missing lady."

"Humph." Luty contented herself with giving Hatchet a good frown and then turned her attention to Mrs. Jeffries. "What do ya want me to start on?"

Mrs. Jeffries had already thought about that. Luty was one of the wealthiest women in London. She socialized with stockbrokers, bankers and industrial leaders. Her contacts in the city were legendary, and, most important, Luty knew who would talk and who wouldn't. "Find out what you can about the victim's financial situation."

"What about this Neville Grant feller?" Luty queried. "Underhill was killed at his house."

"By all means, Luty," Mrs. Jeffries said. "Find out what you can about all of them."

"Includin' the visitin' Americans?"

"Oh yes, we mustn't leave anyone out," she replied.

"Do ya want me to start on the pubs and the cabbies?" Smythe asked.

"Actually, I'd prefer you find out what you can about the victim. It's too bad we don't know where he lived or anything else about the man, but I think it's important we find out as much as possible."

Smythe drummed his fingers lightly on the

table, thinking. "I can nip out tonight and find out a bit about 'im from the locals. Believe me, the news of a suspicious death like that'll already be makin' the rounds of the local pubs."

"You just want an excuse to go out drinking," Betsy charged. "It's not fair, either. The women in the household can't go out looking for information at night —"

"Oh yes, we can," Luty declared. "I've got my peacemaker out in the carriage —"

"Really, madam," Hatchet interrupted. "I do wish you'd leave that wretched gun at home. We're not in the Old West. Carrying a weapon is illegal here. This is a civilized country."

Luty snorted. "Civilized? Cow patties! If you're so dang blasted civilized, how come we always got murders to solve? You ain't any more civilized than I am. You've just got a fancier accent."

"That's not true, lass," Smythe said earnestly, paying no attention to anyone but Betsy. "I only 'ave a pint or two when I go out. But it's important we get started on this —"

"We are gettin' started," Mrs. Goodge interrupted, "and as we don't even know for sure that Underhill's been murdered, I agree with Betsy. It isn't fair that the men can go out and about at night lookin' for clues and we can't."

"But you never leave the kitchen," Wiggins protested.

"That's not the point," the cook replied stoutly.

"Really, everyone," Mrs. Jeffries said firmly. "Let's calm down a moment. There's no need for us to be interrupting one another and making accusations. Betsy" — she looked at the maid — "I quite agree with Smythe. It is important that we get started right away. We are investigating two possibly separate matters. If he can find out a few more facts about either situation, I think he ought to go." She glanced at Wiggins. "But I quite agree with Mrs. Goodge as well. It isn't fair that a female can't walk the city streets at night the way a man does. Now, can we please put our attention back to the immediate problems at hand?"

"I know what I'll be doin' tomorrow," the cook said. "I'll be getting my sources primed and while I'm at it, I'll find out what I can about Irene Simmons."

"What do ya want me to do?" Wiggins asked.

"Get as much information as you can from the servants in the Grant house. Find out who was there, what their relationships to one another are and if any of them had a reason for wanting Underhill dead," she said crisply. "Also, see if any of the staff knows anything about Irene Simmons."

"Cor blimey." Wiggins blinked in surprise at the enormity of his task. Then he saw the teasing glint in the housekeeper's eyes. "Oh, I get it. Find out what I can."

"That's right." She laughed.

"What'll you be doin', Hepzibah?" Luty asked curiously.

"To begin with, I shall wait up for the inspector and find out what he's learned this evening," Mrs. Jeffries said. "Tomorrow, I do believe I'll make a couple of calls."

"To who?" Smythe asked.

"Dr. Bosworth and Nanette Lanier."

"I can see why you want to talk to the good doctor," Hatchet said, "but why are you going to see Miss Lanier? Hasn't she already told you everything she knows about Miss Simmons's disappearance?"

"Indeed she has." Mrs. Jeffries smiled. "But I want to find out what she knows about James Underhill."

Witherspoon's ears were ringing by the time he finished taking Neville Grant's statement. The man didn't believe in speaking below a roar. He winced as the drawing room door slammed shut violently behind Grant.

"He wasn't very helpful, was he, sir?" Barnes asked, glancing down at his notebook. "Perhaps one of the others will be more forthcoming."

"Excuse me, sir." Constable Martin stuck his head into the room. "But the American gentleman wants to know if he and his wife can leave now."

"Could you just send them in here, please?" the inspector instructed. "I'd like to take their statements before they go."

"Yes, sir," the constable replied.

"You're going to interview them together, sir?"

"I'm not sure I ought to be questioning them at all." Witherspoon rubbed his eyes and fought back a yawn. "They've probably got nothing to do with the fellow's death, even if it is a murder. Neville Grant told us they only arrived from America recently, so I don't see how they could have disliked Underhill enough to poison the fellow."

A few moments later, Constable Martin ushered in the Modeans. The inspector introduced himself and Barnes. Tyrell Modean — a tall, dark-haired man with gray sprinkled at his temples and a rugged, tan complexion — was a good ten years older than his beautiful, auburn-haired wife. Lydia Modean wore a bronze-colored day gown that rustled faintly as she crossed the room. The dress was simple with only a decorative fichu of cream lace at the base of her slender throat. But from the cut of the fabric and the way it fitted against her slender frame, it was obviously expensive, even to Witherspoon's less-than-experienced eyes. She wore no jewelry save for an ornately filagreed gold wedding band. The inspector noted her husband wore one just like hers.

When she spoke, his surprise was obvious. "You're English?" he asked. He'd assumed that, like her husband, she was from America.

"Born in Bristol," she replied with a slight smile.

"Excuse me, Inspector, but how long is this going to take?" Tyrell asked. "It's been quite an ordeal for both of us."

"I appreciate that," Witherspoon answered, "but there are a few questions I need to ask. I'll be as quick as possible. Why don't you both have a seat?" He gestured towards the settee.

Modean looked for a moment as though he were going to refuse, then he sighed, took his wife's arm and gallantly seated her before sitting down himself. "What do you want to know? All we can tell you is what we saw."

"That'll be fine, sir. Do go ahead."

"We'd just sat down to have tea when all of a sudden, Underhill started making these noises, kind of a coughing sound. At first I thought he'd swallowed the wrong way or was just coughing to clear out his throat. Then I realized the poor devil was choking. I jumped up and tried to help." He shrugged defeatedly. "Slapped him on the back and got his collar undone, but nothing seemed to do any good. He just kept wheezing and coughing and making these god-awful noises. I thought he must be having a fit of some kind. His body was jerking so hard he fell off the settee. We got him onto his back, but that didn't do any good either. He just thrashed about for a few minutes and then died."

"I see," Witherspoon said slowly. "Was today the first time you'd met James Underhill?"

"No." Modean shook his head. "I'd met him a number of years ago. We didn't really travel in the same circles, but I had run across him before."

"James Underhill introduced the two of us," Lydia Modean put in quickly. "It was several years ago. Tyrell bought some Flemish watercolors from him."

"You're an art dealer, sir?" Witherspoon asked, thinking him a gallery owner from America.

Modean laughed. "I'm a businessman, Inspector. I've a number of irons in the fire back home. Banking, hotels, investments. My vocation is making money, but my great love is art. That's why we're here. I'm negotiating with Mr. Grant to buy three Caldararos."

"Mr. Underhill was an art dealer?" the inspector commented.

"I wouldn't really say that." Modean leaned back against the cushions. "I think 'art dealer' is a bit more formal for what he actually did. The man didn't own a gallery or anything like that, Inspector. He's more what one would call an art broker. By that I mean that he seemed to always know who was buying and who was selling."

"Was Mr. Underhill involved in your negotiations with Mr. Grant?" Witherspoon asked.

"Absolutely not," Modean replied bluntly. "I don't know why Underhill was here today, but it had nothing to do with us." He shot his wife a quick glance. "I just assumed he was a guest of the Grants."

"I see," the inspector murmured. "You were invited for tea?"

"Right. But as Grant and I had business to discuss, Mrs. Grant asked us to come early."

"Exactly what time did you arrive, sir?" Barnes asked.

"I'm not sure."

"Four o'clock, dear," Lydia said. "You and Mr. Grant joined us in the garden about four-fifteen."

Witherspoon wasn't sure precisely what he ought to be asking. It was decidedly awkward questioning people when one wasn't even sure a murder had taken place. "So Mr. and Mrs. Grant were there, as were the two of you. Anyone else?"

It was Lydia who answered. "Helen Collier, Mrs. Grant's sister, was also there, as was Arthur Grant and, of course, Mr. Underhill."

"Arthur Grant?" The inspector vaguely recalled seeing a pale, fidgety young fellow when he'd first arrived. "Is he Mr. Grant's grandson?"

Lydia's eyes sparkled with amusement. "Arthur is his son, Inspector. By his first wife."

"Ah, I see. Well, I suppose Mr. Arthur Grant's antecedents are really neither here nor there."

"Inspector," Tyrell said, "I don't really know what else my wife or I can tell you. We arrived here at about four, I spent ten minutes in the study with Mr. Grant discussing business, then we sat in the garden with the others until tea was served. We'd only been in the drawing room a few moments before Underhill died. It was a perfectly ordinary, civil, if somewhat boring afternoon. Now, if you don't mind, it's been a rather trying day. I'd like to take my wife back to the hotel."

Witherspoon concentrated hard, trying to think if there was something else he ought to ask, but nothing came to mind. "Of course, sir."

Modean and his wife stood up. She sagged against him gently and he put his arm around her shoulders. "If you need to ask us anything else, we'll be at your disposal. We're at the Alexandra in Knightsbridge."

It was quite late by the time the inspector came home that night, but Mrs. Jeffries waited up for him. She took his hat and coat. "I dare say, sir, you must be exhausted. Wiggins and Smythe told us what happened."

"I am a bit tired," he admitted.

"Would you care for some tea before you retire, sir?" she asked. "I've just made a fresh pot."

"That would be lovely, Mrs. Jeffries," Witherspoon agreed eagerly.

"Let's go into the drawing room, shall we?" The housekeeper led the way, clucking sympathetically as she ushered him into his favorite chair and poured his tea.

"I say, Mrs. Jeffries, I went out in such a rush after Miss Lanier's visit that I forgot to ask if there was any word from Lady Cannonberry."

Lady Ruth Cannonberry was their neighbor — a very special friend of the household and, most important, the inspector. She'd been gone now for more than a week on a duty visit to relatives. Inspector Witherspoon missed her dreadfully. "We had a short note saying she'd arrived safely but her plans hadn't changed." Mrs. Jeffries replied. "She'll be back next week."

Mrs. Jeffries continued. "Now, sir. What do you think has happened? Wiggins and Smythe both seemed to think you'd decided this Mr. Underhill had been murdered."

"I'm not certain of that," Witherspoon replied. "But the death was suspicious enough that I began an immediate investigation."

"Yes," she agreed, watching him carefully. "Wiggins told us about Dr. Bosworth's idea. What do you think, sir? Was the man poisoned?" She was quite certain that Bosworth was right, but her main goal right at the moment wasn't to establish the facts in the case — it was to get her employer talking.

"We won't know for sure until after the post-mortem." Witherspoon took a sip of tea, sighed in satisfaction and leaned back in his chair. He closed his eyes.

Alarmed, Mrs. Jeffries quickly said, "What do your instincts tell you, sir?" She firmly squashed the nagging guilt that crept up on her. The poor man was tired. His face was pale, his thin brown hair disheveled and behind his spectacles, his eyes were red-rimmed with fatigue. Even his mustache seemed to droop in weariness.

"Huh?" He blinked. "Oh, sorry, must have dozed off. What did you say?"

"I asked what your instincts told you about this case, sir."

He hesitated. Unlike his housekeeper, he wasn't certain he trusted his instincts all that much. Sometimes they played him false.

"Come now, sir, you mustn't be modest with me. I know you must have some feel for what happened to James Underhill. You're far too brilliant a detective not to have sensed something from the atmosphere surrounding the man's death. Please do tell me."

Pleased by her faith in him, he smiled. Perhaps he was simply tired tonight. It had been rather a long day. His "inner voice" or instincts were really quite sound. Quite sound, indeed. After all, as she'd just reminded him, he was a brilliant detective. One of Scotland Yard's finest. He'd solved any number of tricky murders. "Perhaps I shouldn't say this, but it's my considered opinion that the man was murdered. As a matter of fact, I'm sure of it."

"How very astute of you, sir." She reached for her cup. "Do go on."

Suddenly, the inspector wasn't as tired as he'd been only a few moments ago. "Well, I must say, one of the things that led me to my conclusion was the way the rest of the guests in the house behaved," he explained eagerly. "Not one of them seemed in the least upset that he was actually dead. As a matter of fact, they were more annoyed at being inconvenienced than anything else. That's always a pertinent clue, I think.

78

Whether or not people actually cared about the victim. I sensed that no one really liked James Underhill and it's often been my experience that people who aren't well liked frequently end up murdered."

"So you questioned everyone?"

"I took statements from the guests and had the police constables question the servants."

Mrs. Jeffries took a sip from her own cup. "According to those statements, exactly what happened this afternoon?"

Witherspoon yawned. "Well, just as Mrs. Grant was getting ready to pour the tea, James Underhill popped some peppermints in his mouth and then appeared to choke. By the time the others in the room realized the man was having serious difficulties, it was too late to do anything for him. Though mind you, if Dr. Bosworth is correct, there wouldn't have been anything anyone could do for the poor chap."

"I see," she said softly. There were a dozen questions she needed to ask, but she couldn't decide what was the best way to proceed.

The clock struck the hour and she started, realizing that one of the reasons she couldn't think straight was that it was late. When she glanced over at the inspector, he was slumped back against the seat, his cup and saucer rested precariously on his lap, and his eyes were closed.

Rising quietly, she plucked the china out of harm's way and placed it on the table beside the inspector's chair. Gently, she shook him. "Sir," she whispered. "I do believe you'd better retire for the evening."

Mrs. Jeffries was up and gone from the house before the others had stirred. The hansom let her out at the junction where Newgate Street meets Cheapside. She smiled at the statue of Sir Robert Peel, the founder of the police force, and fancied for a moment that he smiled back at her, approving her actions. Then she straightened her spine, nimbly stepped off the hackney island and made her way down Cheapside.

The area was quiet at this time of the morning, though shortly it would be swarming with pedestrians hurrying to work, hacks vying for fares and omnibuses disgorging shoppers and clerks. She drew her cloak tighter against the morning chill as she walked toward Cutters Lane. Turning the corner, her footsteps slowed as she surveyed the shops lining both sides of the ancient, narrow lane. Nanette's shop was on the other side of the street, halfway down the block.

The shop itself was still dark and the awning rolled back against the building. But on the floor above, Mrs. Jeffries noticed the windows were open and the blinds up.

Moving quickly but quietly, Mrs. Jeffries crossed the road and stopped in front of the shop. LANIER'S was written in delicate script lettering on the front door. She turned and stared at the goods displayed in the front window.

Elegant hats were exhibited artfully on a three-tiered brass hatstand. Below them a display of gloves, both two-button and four-button and one spectacular twelve-button pair embroidered with red silk, were artfully displayed on a bed of white velvet. The window itself was draped with a mantle of blue crepe de chine, puffed elegantly around the edges to give one the sensation of looking at a painting. From the looks of things, Mrs. Jeffries thought, Nanette Lanier was doing quite well.

She glanced along the building front, looking for the entrance into the flats above the shop. A door, the same gray color as the stone of the building, was at the far end.

As there was no knocker or bell, Mrs. Jeffries made a fist and banged on the wood. Several times.

"A moment, *s'il vous plait!*" an irritated voice shouted.

Footsteps sounded on stairs and then the door was flung open. "I have told you a thousand times . . ." Nanette's voice trailed off as she saw Mrs. Jeffries standing in front of her. "*Mon dieu,* I thought you were someone else," she apologized quickly and moved back. "You have zee news already! Please, tell me it is good news you bring me."

"We haven't found your friend yet," Mrs. Jeffries said calmly as she stepped inside. The foyer was so small there was barely room for the two women. "But I must talk with you."

"But of course. Please, let's go upstairs," Nanette said. "It's more comfortable."

Mrs. Jeffries followed her up the narrow, steep stairs to the first-floor landing. Nanette led the way through an open door into a small sitting room. Like its owner, the room was elegant, unusual and decidedly French. There was very little furniture — only a love seat upholstered in pale green damask and a matching chair. A small table, polished to a high gloss and holding only a crystal vase with a rose sat next to it. An exquisite blue-and-green woven rug covered the floor. Nanette gestured to the love seat. "Please sit down. Would you like some café au lait?"

"No, thank you," Mrs. Jeffries said politely. She sat down on the settee.

Nanette's expression was speculative as she took a seat in the chair. "Why have you come?"

"Do you know a man named James Underhill?" Mrs. Jeffries asked. She watched her quarry carefully.

Nanette's body jerked ever so slightly. "I have heard zhis name, yes. Why? What has he to do with Irene's disappearance?"

"He was murdered yesterday afternoon."

Nanette gasped involuntarily. "He is dead?"

"Oh yes, he's quite dead. According to witnesses, he may have been poisoned," Mrs. Jeffries said briskly. She'd deliberately been blunt. The fact that she still wasn't certain Underhill's death was a murder hadn't deterred her from seeing what kind of reaction she'd get from Nanette. "He died at the Grant house."

"Mon dieu," Nanette whispered. *"C'est impossible."*

"I'm afraid it's quite possible," Mrs. Jeffries said. "He popped a peppermint in his mouth and a few moments later, he was gone. Now I want to know what's going on. What, precisely, is your relationship to this man and, most important, when was the last time you saw him?" She was certain she was right. It wasn't that Mrs. Jeffries didn't believe in coincidences. She did. She'd seen them happen all the time, but she didn't think there was anything coincidental between the death of James Underhill and the alleged disappearance of Irene Simmons. At first, she'd not been sure that Nanette had even known the dead man. But after seeing her reaction to his name and glimpsing the wariness in her eyes, she realized that the events were connected.

Nanette said nothing for a moment. Finally, she sighed and looked toward the open window. "I used to love him."

"Used to love him?"

Nanette nodded slowly, her gaze still locked on the window, her eyes unfocused. "Zhen I found out what kind of a man he really was" — her voice trembled — "and I stopped loving him. I made myself stop loving him." She wiped at a tear that rolled down her cheek.

"When was the last time you saw him?" Mrs. Jeffries asked again.

"Yesterday afternoon." Nanette sniffed and

wiped her cheeks. "He was here right after zee noon meal."

"Why?" Mrs. Jeffries queried. "It certainly doesn't sound like you had any love left for the man."

"I didn't," Nanette said hastily. "I hated him. I've hated him for a long time."

"Then why was he here?"

"Because I had no choice. If I wanted any peace, I had to see him. He came to get his payment . . . it was already a week late." She leapt to her feet and began pacing the room.

Mrs. Jeffries ignored the histrionics. This was starting to sound interesting. Despite what the romantics would have one believe about love making the world go round, it had often been Mrs. Jeffries's experience that as a motive for murder, money was usually the culprit more often than affairs of the heart. "What kind of payment might this be?" she asked. "A loan, perhaps?"

"A loan? From Underhill?" She stopped next to the window and laughed bitterly. "*Mais, non.* He was too mean to loan anyone money." Nanette turned and stared out onto the street. Her back was ramrod straight and her arms held stiffly against her sides. Her hands were balled into fists so tightly her knuckles turned white.

Sensing that the Frenchwoman was waging some terrible internal battle, Mrs. Jeffries simply waited patiently, saying nothing.

Nanette sighed deeply. "James was black-mailing me."

"How long has it been going on?"

"Almost from the day I opened zhis shop." She turned and shrugged. "I've told you now. I suppose you'll want to tell zee inspector. Underhill is dead. I had a reason to kill him, *non?*"

"Nanette," Mrs. Jeffries said gently, "why don't you tell me the whole story?"

"I'm afraid it's an old one, madam. A foolish young girl. A clever man and voilà, I am in chains for zee rest of my life." Nanette smiled wearily. "Two years ago, I was uh . . . given a painting by a gentleman friend. It was a nice oil painting. Quite old and very pretty. It was a picture of a city along a river somewhere in Italy. I didn't zink it was very valuable, but I liked it. My friend died. He was quite an . . . er, elderly gentleman. At his funeral, I met James Underhill. We were immediately attracted to one another, or so I thought." She shrugged her shoulders. "I was alone in zee world. I wanted to leave my employment and make a better life for myself. James and I began seeing each other. Within a short while, he began asking questions about zee painting. He told me it was worth a lot of money and he offered to sell it for me." She waved her arm in a wide arc. "Zat's where I got zee money for all zhis, zee shop, zee lease hold on zee building. Zee money for zee stock. I was so happy. I opened my shop and I had my lover."

"Selling one painting got you that much money?"

Nanette laughed bitterly. "The painting was a Caldararo."

"Ah, now I understand." Mrs. Jeffries was no expert, but even she knew the value of a Genoa Caldararo painting. The great sixteenth-century Florentine artist had done fewer than a dozen canvases before his untimely death. His work was valuable not simply because of its brilliance, but because of its scarcity.

"A few months after I'd opened," Nanette continued, "after I'd spent every *sou*, James took me to dinner at a beautiful restaurant. There was wine and music and fresh flowers on zee table. I thought he was going to propose. I know such a thing is unusual. A man usually asks for a lady's hand in private, after zee formalities are completed with zee family. But I had no family, no papa for James to ask permission. So when he took such care to make zee dinner so special, so . . . so . . . well, I was a silly, romantic fool. He took me to zhat restaurant not to please me, but to make sure I wouldn't make a public scene. As you've guessed, James didn't ask me to marry him. Instead, he announced zat zee painting I'd sold was a forgery. An excellent one, but a forgery nonezeeless. It was worthless."

"But that wasn't your fault," Mrs. Jeffries exclaimed.

"Zat didn't matter," Nanette replied. "If zee new owner of zee Caldararo found out it was worthless, he would sue me. Perhaps even have me arrested. James had made sure it was my name on zee bill of sale."

"But he'd been the one to broker the painting."

"He'd merely claim he'd been duped as well," Nanette replied. "I am a foreigner, Mrs. Jeffries. I was a maid before I opened my shop. James Underhill was from an ancient and honorable family. That makes a difference in zhis world. Believe me, Mrs. Jeffries, if I could have found a way to put zee blame on him, I would have. But zee truth was, I couldn't afford a lawsuit. Zee man who bought zee Caldararo was a rich collector. He could ruin me."

"I take it Underhill wanted money for his silence."

Nanette nodded. "He said he wasn't going to be unreasonable," she said. "He'd take monthly payments. Every bit of profit zhis place has earned has gone into his pocket, not mine. I've paid well for his silence."

"And now he's dead."

"Yes," Nanette admitted. "He's dead. I won't have to pay him again. So, as you can see, I had a reason to want him dead."

"I've a suspicion you weren't the only one," Mrs. Jeffries mused thoughtfully. She considered the method used to murder Underhill. Nanette could have done it. Easily. But had she? "Nanette, there's one more thing I need to know. What connection did Irene Simmons have with Underhill?"

Chapter 4

"It were murder, all right," Wiggins told the others. They were gathered around the table at Upper Edmonton Gardens. As planned, they'd met back there for an early midday meal.

"I done just like you told me, Mrs. Jeffries," he said to the housekeeper. "I went straight into the station. The copper at the desk tried to stop me, but Constable Barnes was comin' down the stairs and when he 'eard me natterin' on with that tale of needin' to give the inspector 'is spectacles, he took me straight up. The inspector had just come back from a meetin' with the chief inspector." He leaned forward, his expression as solemn as an undertaker's. "Underhill was poisoned. Our inspector's got the case."

"Pinched the inspector's spectacles, did ya, Hepzibah?" Luty cackled. "You ain't pulled that trick in a long while."

"I did think it rather prudent to have an excuse at hand so that one of us could see the inspector this morning," she replied. "Admittedly, I haven't had to use that particular ruse in a good while. But it has stood us in good stead. We now

88

know that Underhill's death really was murder." She turned her attention back to the footman. "Were you able to find out anything else?"

Wiggins frowned. "No. Right after I gave him 'is spectacles, he 'ad to dash off with Constable Barnes. I 'eard 'im tellin' the sergeant they was goin' back to the Grant house to ask some more questions."

"Excellent work, Wiggins," Mrs. Jeffries said. "I'm delighted our assumptions were correct."

"Before you lot start on about your precious murder," Betsy said hastily, "I've got something to report. I've found out a bit about Irene Simmons. It's right interestin' if I do say so myself."

" 'Ow'd you do that?" Wiggins demanded. "It's not even gone on eleven o'clock."

"I was up and out early," Betsy retorted.

"And you left without a bite of breakfast," Smythe chided. "You'll make yourself ill if you start missin' meals, lass. Besides, I don't know that you ought to be dashin' off anywhere without lettin' someone know where you're goin'."

"Betsy did let me know where she was going," Mrs. Jeffries said quickly. She didn't want an argument to break out between Smythe and Betsy. The maid was an independent sort and the coachman, for a variety of reasons, tended to be ridiculously overly protective of her. "Please do go on, Betsy. What have you found out today?"

"Well, I was going to go over to the Grant

house and have a go at the servants there, see if any of them might have seen Irene. But when I got there the place was dark as a tomb. It was still so early, you see. I didn't want to waste the morning so I nipped over to the Battersea Bridge and walked up the river a bit."

Smythe, who'd just taken a drink of tea, choked. "You was walkin' along the river? By yourself? At the crack of dawn?"

"Oh, Smythe, don't be such an old wo— silly," she sputtered, quickly changing the last word from "woman" to "silly" before she could cause offense to any of the three elderly ladies at the table. "I was perfectly safe. There's police constables about on Cheyne Walk."

"What put it into your head to do that?" Mrs. Goodge asked curiously.

"There's artists there," Betsy explained, ignoring the disapproving scowl on Smythe's face. "They go to paint the river in the morning light. I've seen them. This morning there was two of them. One was down by the Chelsea Pier, but he was useless. He'd never heard of anyone called Irene Simmons. Got a bit nasty when I asked him too." She snorted delicately. "He didn't much like having his painting interrupted, not that there was all that much to interrupt if you ask me. Fellow wasn't very good. The river looked like an oily old fat snake with a bad case of the pox, and that's what I told him when he got all shirty with me too," she said indignantly. "But the second painter was a bit more useful."

90

"He knew Irene?" Mrs. Jeffries asked.

"No, but he knew where I might find out something. He sent me along to a cafe in Soho. I had some really good luck there. The first person I spoke to was able to tell me something. Seems Irene's quite well known as a model. Anyway, Harriet — she's the woman who works the counter at the cafe — told me that Gaspar Morante had been in a few weeks earlier. He had some sketches with him which he was showing to another artist. Harriet couldn't remember exactly what the sketches were, but they had a woman in them. Harriet picks up a bit of money every now and then posing, so she asked Morante if he was going to do a painting of the picture he'd sketched and if he was, did he need a model." She leaned forward eagerly. "And you'll never guess what Morante told her. He said he was going to use the model that had posed for the sketches."

"I take it the model was Irene Simmons," Hatchet finished.

Betsy nodded. "Right."

"Gaspar Morante. Sounds like a foreigner," Mrs. Goodge muttered. "Probably one of them dark, swarthy types that are up to no good. Where have I heard that name before?"

"He's the one that give Irene her first job," Betsy replied eagerly. "And that's what's important. According to Harriet, Morante would probably know everyone who'd ever hired Irene." She paused to take a breath and realized that the others at the table were gazing at her blankly. "Don't you understand? Morante might have some idea of who wrote her the note."

"Betsy," Mrs. Jeffries warned. "The note luring Irene to the Grant house was probably quite bogus. We've no idea why it was written. It might not have anything to do with an artist . . ." She faltered as she realized the maid's reasoning might be right on the mark. Whoever wrote that note knew that Irene was a model. That might be common knowledge at a cafe in Soho, but it probably wasn't information that was known outside of a rather small circle. Irene Simmons didn't advertise herself as a model. She obtained work through word-of-mouth. Besides, Betsy needed to be encouraged, not discouraged. She and Hatchet didn't have all that much to work with in the way of clues. This idea, weak that it might be, was certainly better than nothing. "On the other hand, you're probably on to something here. Whoever wrote Irene that note knew she was available for work."

"That's what I thought," Betsy agreed. "I know it's not much. This man might not have seen Irene in weeks and probably won't know anything about her at all. But unless Hatchet's come up with some more ideas, it's all I've got."

"I'm afraid I haven't," Hatchet admitted.

"So what are you going to do now?" Mrs. Goodge asked. "Track down this Spaniard?"

"Morante's got a studio in Soho," Betsy replied. "It's right near the cafe. I'll go there right after we finish up here."

"By yourself?" Smythe blurted out before he could stop himself.

Betsy rolled her eyes. "It'll be broad daylight. I'll be just fine. Now stop interrupting or we'll be here all morning. I'm not the only one who's got something to report. Mrs. Jeffries has been to see Nanette. I want to hear what she found out." She pretended to be more annoyed than she really was. She loved her independence, but she also liked knowing that there were people who cared about her.

"Would you like me to come with you to the man's studio?" Hatchet offered.

Luty snickered. "What's the matter, Hatchet, you worried that Betsy's gittin' the jump on ya?"

"Don't be absurd, madam." Hatchet sniffed. "That would be childish."

Betsy thought about it for a moment. If she said yes, then she'd be admitting that going out in the middle of the afternoon was too dangerous for a woman to handle on her own. That could cause lots of future problems with a certain overly protective male of her acquaintance. On the other hand, she hadn't liked the way some of the men at the cafe had looked at her this morning. "No, that's all right. I'll take care to be cautious. I always do. But thank you for offering."

"That's quite all right." Hatchet inclined his head formally. "However, do let me know if you need my assistance. I'm well aware that there are some parts of this city where it isn't safe for a young woman to be alone, even in broad daylight."

"Did you find out anything else?" Luty asked.

"Not really." Betsy covered her mouth as she stifled a yawn.

"I think you've done quite well." Mrs. Jeffries reached for the teapot. "As Betsy mentioned, I went along to see Nanette Lanier this morning."

"Is her shop nice, then?" Wiggins asked eagerly. He didn't give a fig about women's hats, but he did want to know everything he could about the lovely Frenchwoman.

"Very." With a wry smile, Mrs. Jeffries picked up her cup and took a dainty sip. "I'd rather expected a more modest establishment."

Mrs. Goodge, noting the half-smile on the housekeeper's lips, eyed her speculatively. "Just how posh is this shop?"

"Let me put it this way, if I may," Mrs. Jeffries said. "The cost of one pair of evening gloves would be enough to provide you or I with clothing for the entire year. Nanette wasn't jesting when she told us she had the latest hat styles directly from Paris. She does. With French prices too, I might add."

"Cor blimey," Smythe exclaimed. " 'Ow in a month of bloomin' Sundays did a maid get the capital to open a fancy place like that? She must be rich as sin."

"She's not rich," Mrs. Jeffries remarked.

"Doesn't the shop do well?" Hatchet asked.

"Very. If it weren't for one minor detail, I suspect Nanette would be making a handsome living from the place. As it is, she can barely make ends meet." Mrs. Jeffries smiled grimly. "Despite the success of her business, Nanette Lanier's financial position is quite precarious. You see, she's being blackmailed."

"Blackmailed!" Luty echoed eagerly. "By who?"

"James Underhill."

Smythe whistled softly. Betsy's pretty mouth parted in surprise, Wiggins's eyes widened to the size of treacle tarts and even Hatchet was taken aback.

The only one who didn't appear shocked was Luty. "I ain't surprised," she commented. "Never did much believe in coincidences. I figured Underhill dyin' and Irene Simmons disappearin' had to be all muddled up together somehow or other."

"How very astute of you, madam," Hatchet said sarcastically. "Unfortunately, the rest of us aren't nearly as perceptive as yourself, so if you don't mind, can we let Mrs. Jeffries go on with her report?"

Luty, to her credit, didn't respond to her butler's sarcasm, though she did snicker a little as soon as he'd turned his attention back to the housekeeper.

"Now, as I was saying," Mrs. Jeffries continued briskly, "Underhill was blackmailing Nanette."

"Why didn't Nanette tell us?" Betsy asked,

feeling horribly confused. Pity, really, she had a lot of plans of her own for doing some discreet digging about both the murder and Irene.

"Because she didn't think her problem of being blackmailed by Underhill had anything to do with Irene's disappearance," Mrs. Jeffries explained.

"Did Underhill know Irene?" Wiggins asked.

"Oh, yes. As a matter of fact, Underhill got Irene her first modeling position."

"But Nanette told us that Irene got started 'cause Gaspar Morante 'ad walked in and seen 'er behind the counter." Smythe raised an eyebrow. "She's changin' 'er story now?"

"Morante was the artist," Mrs. Jeffries said. "But he didn't walk into the shop. As far as Nanette knows, he's never been in. It was Underhill who got Irene the work. He spotted the girl when he went to collect his money from Nanette."

"Why didn't she tell us the truth right from the start?" Wiggins complained. "All this lyin' is gettin' me confused."

"It is annoying," Mrs. Jeffries agreed. "But I think you'll understand when you hear the rest."

Inspector Witherspoon didn't like to be unkind, but Arthur Grant reminded him a bit of a nervous rabbit. The fellow couldn't seem to sit still for more than two seconds. His behaviour was in marked contrast to his stepmother's.

Regal as a queen, Mary Grant sat on the settee

next to her sister. She hadn't so much as batted an eyelash when the inspector had told them that their late guest had been poisoned. Her expression had softened momentarily at Helen's involuntary gasp upon hearing the news. But after a quick, sympathetic glance at her sister, she'd turned back to stare at the inspector and Barnes, her expresssion calm and composed. "How very unfortunate," she murmured. "What kind of poison was it?"

Witherspoon hesitated. There was no reason not to tell them. All three of them had witnessed the victim's death. They'd seen how fast he'd died. As there were very few poisons that acted that quickly, there was no point in trying to keep it a secret. "Cyanide."

"I don't see why you've come back." Arthur whined and chewed on his lower lip. "We told you everything last night."

"I'm sure you did, sir," Witherspoon said patiently, "but at the time, we didn't know Mr. Underhill was a victim of foul play."

"Are you sure you're not mistaken?" Mary Grant asked.

"I assure you, madam," Witherspoon said. "The postmortem was quite thorough. Cyanide is not difficult to detect."

"I don't doubt that, Inspector," she replied. "What I meant was, are you sure it was foul play? Underhill could just as well have committed suicide as been murdered."

"James would never have taken his own life."

Helen sobbed. "He had too much to live for. We were going to announce our engagement."

"Don't be ridiculous, Helen," Mary chided her sister, gentling her expression a fraction. "Your engagement was hardly official. I don't think you ought to be telling all and sundry you were his fiancée. It doesn't look very nice, especially as he had the bad taste to die in our drawing room during high tea."

"You don't understand. I loved him." Helen shoved a handkerchief over her mouth. "And he loved me."

Witherspoon looked at Barnes, hoping the constable could give him some clue as to what to do next. A woman crying always made him feel he ought to help in some way. But Barnes appeared unperturbed and merely continued scribbling in his little brown notebook.

Mary sighed patiently, the way one did when dealing with a foolish child who refused to believe that three pieces of cake would make one ill. "I'm sure it's nice for you to think he was in love with you," she said. "But dearest, do be sensible. You didn't really know him all that well. The poor man might have been upset or depressed about any number of things."

"I've known him since before Papa died," Helen cried. "So I think I would know whether or not he was depressed, and he wasn't. He was happy."

Mary's anguish for her sister was reflected on her face. "Please, Helen, don't upset yourself . . ."

"Upset myself! Don't be absurd. My fiancé is dead. Of course I'm upset. Anyone would be. Anyone except you, and that's because you've no feelings," Helen flung at her sister. "None at all. James and I were going to be married. He told me so right before he died." With that, she leapt to her feet and ran from the room.

Mary Grant sighed and turned her attention back to the police. "You'll have to forgive Miss Collier," she said formally. "She's not herself today. Now, sir, will you please answer my question? Helen's hysterics aside, isn't it possible that Mr. Underhill chose to take his own life?"

The police had considered and rejected the idea of suicide.

"It's a bad way to go, ma'am," Barnes supplied. "If he wanted to kill himself, he'd have likely chosen an easier way of doing it." The constable could think of a half dozen better ways of dying other than choking your life out with cyanide.

"I see." Mary swallowed heavily. "All right, Inspector, perhaps you'd better get on with this. Ask your questions."

"Er, if you don't mind," Witherspoon ventured, "I'd quite like to speak to young Mr. Grant first."

Confused, Mary stared at him, then smiled slightly as she realized precisely what he meant. "Oh, I understand. You want to question him alone."

"That's right." Witherspoon was too much of

a gentleman to ask her to leave. "Is there another room we can use? Perhaps your husband's study?"

She got to her feet and started for the door. "That won't be necessary. You can speak to him here." With that, she nodded and swept out of the room, slamming the door ever so slightly as she left.

Witherspoon turned his attention to the young man, searching for just the right words to calm the fellow so he could get some answers out of him.

But apparently, Arthur had gotten over his nervousness.

He was grinning from ear to ear. "You got the old girl ruffled." He chuckled.

"Ruffled? I'm afraid I don't understand, sir."

"She tried to hide it, but she was as angry as a scalded cat." Arthur snickered. "She didn't like being asked to leave. Hurt her pride, that did."

"I assure you, that wasn't my intention, sir." Gracious, the inspector thought, was everyone in this household peculiar? "Now, if you don't mind, I'd like to get this over with. How long have you known James Underhill?"

The mention of the dead man wiped the grin off Arthur's thin face. "A good number of years. I don't know exactly." He began drumming his fingers against the sides of his thighs.

"How did you meet him, then?"

"I didn't," Arthur sputtered. "I mean, he's the sort of person who's always been about the place."

"I'm sorry," the inspector pressed. "But I don't understand."

"He was a friend of the family," Arthur said quickly. "He's been around for ages. Absolutely ages."

"But I got the distinct impression from your mother . . ."

"Stepmother," Arthur corrected, interrupting. "She's my stepmother."

Witherspoon raised a placating hand. "All right, your stepmother — that Mr. Underhill was merely a business acquaintance."

"He is," Arthur explained worriedly. "I mean, he was. Oh, dash it all, I'm not explaining it very well."

The inspector agreed. The young man was explaining nothing.

"But you see," Arthur began, "this is deucedly awkward. He's from quite a good family. But they've no money, not anymore. So James had to resort to actually earning his living. Quite awful for him, really."

Witherspoon closed his eyes briefly. "I'm sorry, sir. But what does Mr. Underhill having had to earn a living have to do with how long you'd known the poor man?"

"But I'm telling you," Arthur exclaimed. "That's how we knew him. He's sort of an art dealer. My stepmother first met him a number of years ago. He helped her sell off some very valuable paintings that had been in her family for years. When she married Papa, she recommended he use Underhill to act as a broker when he bought or sold. Papa does dearly love his collection."

"So Mr. Underhill was more an employee of the family rather than a friend?"

Arthur shook his head. "No . . . well . . . but as I said, it was quite awkward sometimes. I mean, before they lost all their money, his family was quite well connected. Quite well off as well." He sighed. "Poor old James was the last of them and now he's dead too."

"Was he here as a friend or an art advisor?" Witherspoon asked. He'd no idea why he thought that point worth clarifying, but he did.

"Yesterday he was here as my guest," Arthur admitted.

"So he is a friend of yours, then?"

"Well, yes, you could say that." Arthur clasped his hands together in his lap. "But we weren't particularly close friends."

"Then why did you invite him for tea?" Barnes asked dryly.

Arthur hesitated a moment before answering. "He asked me to."

"He asked to be invited?" Witherspoon wanted to make sure he understood correctly. This young man was a bit muddled in his answers. In his thinking, as well.

"Oh, yes," Arthur said brightly. "He waylaid me at my club yesterday morning and specifically asked me to invite him to tea."

Witherspoon stared at him speculatively. "Did

he tell you why? Did he give you a reason?"

Arthur shrugged. "Not especially." He leaned forward and dropped his voice to a whisper. "But just between you and me, sir, I think he wanted to see Mrs. Modean. He was quite taken with her."

Betsy quietly opened the back door and slipped out. She glanced around her, making sure that one of the others wasn't lurking about on the small, square back terrace or in the communal gardens directly ahead of her. Satisfied that she was unobserved, she scurried to the side of the house, crept along the walk and out the gate leading to the street. She wasn't being secretive, just cautious. She wouldn't put it past Smythe to try to come with her. Or failing that, she wouldn't put it past the man to put Wiggins up to trailing her. Betsy didn't want or need either of them dogging her heels. She could handle this on her own.

Coming out onto the pavement, she cast one fast look over her shoulder and hurried down the street. She patted the pocket of her short gray wool jacket, making sure she had money enough for a hansom cab if her business kept her out after dark. Reassured by the hefty weight of the coins, she smiled and picked up her step. She had a plan. A plan to find out precisely what had happened to Irene Simmons. Perhaps, she thought, as she hurried to the omnibus stop, she'd find out who murdered James Underhill while she was at it.

Smythe stood in the kitchen and scowled. "What do ya mean, ya don't know where she's gone?"

Wiggins, who was pulling on his boots, shrugged. "But I don't," he said. "After we finished our meetin' I nipped upstairs to get me jacket and when I come down again, everyone was gone."

"I'm still here," Mrs. Goodge said as she came out of the cooling pantry carrying a bag of flour. "And I'll thank you two to get on your way. The grocer's lad should be here any time now and I want to find out if he knows anything. After that I've got a costermonger and the rag and bones man stopping in."

"Have you seen Betsy?" Smythe asked as he and Wiggins edged toward the back hall. "She didn't say she was goin' out so soon, and I was wantin' to make sure she didn't nip off to Soho on 'er own."

Mrs. Goodge allowed a soft smile to play about her lips for a moment. The man was crazy in love with the girl, that was certain. Betsy, whether she'd admit it or not, was just as balmy about him. Too bad the two of them were so pigheaded and stubborn about it. Sometimes Mrs. Goodge felt like giving them both a good cuff around the ears. For every step forward they took, they went two steps back. Love really was wasted on the young. "Don't fret, Smythe. Soho's not the black pit of sin. She'll be fine.

Betsy's got a good head on her shoulders. Go on, now, out with the two of you. We've a murder to solve, and my sources will be here any minute. They'll not talk much with you lot hangin' about. Off with you."

Smythe, knowing when he was beaten, scowled and headed for the back door. "When Betsy gets 'ome," he called over his shoulder to the cook, "ask her to stay put, will ya? I'd like to ask 'er somethin'."

"Are you goin' to ask 'er to the Crystal Palace?" Wiggins asked excitedly. "I 'eard it's the last week for the Photographic Exhibition. I bet she'd love to go. I sure would," he hinted. "There's a diorama and a military band and . . . and . . ."

"Yes, I'm goin' to ask 'er." Smythe grunted irritably as he stepped out the back door. Blast, he didn't like the idea of her going to some studio in Soho. Annoyed that she'd slipped out before he could talk to her, he was also wracked with guilt. He'd planned on taking Betsy to the Palace alone. But he knew how badly Wiggins wanted to go. The lad had talked about the exhibition for days now. Only the boy probably hadn't the money to go before it closed. Wiggins put a good portion of his wages in his post office savings account. Mrs. Jeffries had seen to that, and it was a good thing too. Money slipped through the footman's fingers like water. Smythe was torn. He wanted an evening or an afternoon alone with Betsy, but if he didn't take Wiggins, the boy wouldn't get to go. Blast, Smythe thought as he stomped toward the gate at the side of the house, what good did it do him being rich as sin if he couldn't help his friends? "Why don't ya come with us?"

"Ya mean it?" Wiggins yelped, his face bright with pleasure. "But I really shouldn't . . . it'll cost . . ."

"Don't worry about the cost, lad," Smythe said brusquely as he opened the gate. "I've had a good turn or two at the races lately. It'll be on me. Now, where ya off to?"

Wiggins grinned. "I'm goin' back to the Grant house to see if I can find one of them 'ousemaids. The red-haired one was right nice lookin'. 'Ow about you?"

"Me? Oh, I'll try the pubs and the cabbies in the area," he lied. "See what I can pick up. What time are we meetin' back 'ere?"

"Mrs. Jeffries said right after supper," Wiggins replied. "Luty and Hatchet are supposed to be here too."

They swung around a corner. Smythe started to cross the road. He stopped when Wiggins called to him. "I thought you said you was goin' to the pubs?"

Smythe jerked his chin toward the hansoms lined up on the other side of the busy intersection. "I'm just goin' to 'ave a quick word over there," he replied. "I'll see you back at 'ome tonight."

Wiggins waved and continued on his way, his

mind already on the red-haired housemaid.

Smythe waited till the footman was well up the road before crossing over to one of the hansom cabs. "Do ya know a pub called The Dirty Duck?" he asked the cabbie.

The driver laughed and looked Smythe up and down. "Reckon I do, mate. But it'll cost a bit. It's over by the docks."

"That's all right." Smythe swung himself inside. "I know where it is. But if ya can get me there quick, there'll be an extra bob or two for yer pocket."

Mary Grant regarded the two policemen calmly. If, as her stepson claimed, she'd been "ruffled," the inspector thought, there was certainly no sign of it now.

"Mrs. Grant," he began, "I'd like to ask you a bit about your relationship with Mr. Underhill. I understand from your son . . ."

"My stepson," she corrected. "He's Neville's son, not mine. As to my relationship with James Underhill . . ." She shrugged. "It was purely business."

"Business? But young Mr. Grant claims Underhill had known you and your sister since before you were married to Mr. Neville Grant."

"That's correct," Mary replied. "But it was still basically a business relationship. He helped dispose of my father's art collection when he died."

"Yet he was an invited guest in your house,"

Witherspoon reminded her.

"Only because Arthur asked me to invite him," she replied. "In any case, it wasn't really a social occasion. The Modeans were only here for business reasons. They're hardly the sort of people I would consider friends."

"But I was under the impression" — the inspector cleared his throat — "that Mr. Underhill was your sister's fiancé."

Mary Grant smiled grimly. "This is rather awkward, Inspector. I'm not in the habit of discussing personal business with the police, but given the conversation you've already witnessed between Helen and I, I suppose I've no choice but to explain."

The Inspector wished someone would. His interview with Arthur Grant hadn't made much sense either.

"James Underhill was not Helen's fiancé," Mary said bluntly. "She would like to think they were engaged, but I assure you, they were not."

"How can you be so sure?" Barnes asked softly. He flipped back through the pages of his notebook. "Miss Collier clearly stated that Mr. Underhill and she had discussed the matter of marriage when they were out in the garden yesterday afternoon. And that she'd agreed to wed the man."

She sighed dramatically. "I don't doubt that she said just that. She may actually believe it happened. But the truth is, James hardly spoke to her when we were out in the gardens. Oh, they may have vaguely discussed marriage. James may have even dropped a hint or two about it yesterday afternoon. But an official engagement? No. As I said, our relationship with the man was one of business."

"What about Miss Collier's relationship?" the inspector pressed. She'd been most adamant on the subject, although not particularly coherent. She had been very difficult to question. She'd kept dissolving into tears. Still, the one thing they had managed to get out of her was that she and James Underhill had decided to marry. Yesterday afternoon. Right before Underhill was murdered. The inspector had rather admired the way she'd popped into the drawing room as soon as they'd finished questioning Arthur. Red faced and teary eyed, she'd demanded they listen to her.

"Relationship?" Mary smiled sadly. "The only relationship Helen had with James Underhill was in her imagination. My sister makes her home with us. But she comes and goes as she pleases. I don't particularly know how or why she developed this affection for Mr. Underhill, but I assure you, it wasn't mutual. He wouldn't have proposed to her. Not under any circumstances."

Witherspoon thought that a rather harsh assessment. Miss Collier was past the first blush of youth, but that didn't mean she was unmarriageable. "Why ever not?"

"Because she's no money," Mary replied

bluntly. "No dowry, no property, nothing but a small yearly income which wouldn't be enough to keep her if she didn't live with Neville and I."

"Perhaps Mr. Underhill planned to support her," Barnes suggested dryly.

Mary stared at him a moment and then laughed. "James Underhill loved only one thing in this world, Constable, and it wasn't my sister. It was art. He'd never have married a virtually penniless woman, even if he was in love with her. James was like one of those dreadfully pathetic opium eaters. Only instead of opium, his need was for beauty."

"Not money?" Witherspoon queried.

"Money was only useful to him as a means of acquiring art," she replied.

"Does he have an extensive art collection?"

"Not really." She shrugged. "He couldn't afford any truly valuable paintings, but he fancied himself talented at spotting undiscovered genius in others. James was always picking up pieces here and there on the cheap. His collection is quite extensive in size, but nonetheless quite worthless in value, I assure you."

Witherspoon made a mental note to have a look at Underhill's collection himself. "You've stated your relationship with Mr. Underhill was strictly business, correct?"

"Correct."

"Did you acquiesce to your stepson's request to invite Mr. Underhill to tea because of the pending sale to Mr. Modean?" Witherspoon asked.

"When Arthur asked if he could invite James to tea, I thought it a good idea to have him come. James knows much about what a piece is really worth. Actually, I wanted Neville to have a chat with James before he sold the paintings," Mary explained. "I wasn't sure the American was going to pay what they were really worth. My husband is a bit naive when it comes to art."

Witherspoon tried to hide his surprise. Neville Grant didn't look in the least naive about anything. "Did your husband talk with Mr. Underhill?"

"No," Mary admitted with a sad smile. "There wasn't time. James was late. By the time he arrived, my husband and Mr. Modean had already come to an arrangement."

"You mean that Mr. Modean now owns the paintings?" Witherspoon asked.

"I'm not sure." She stiffened slightly. "Neville refused to discuss it with me."

The inspector didn't know what to ask next. He was getting very muddled, very muddled indeed. But, mindful of his housekeeper's always sound advice, he trusted his "inner voice" and pressed on, asking any question that popped into his head. "Do you know if Mr. Underhill had any enemies?"

"Enemies?" Mary looked amused by the question. "I dare say, sir, he probably had many of them. He wasn't a particularly charming man. I don't think Mrs. Modean liked him all that much, and I'm quite certain her husband had no use for him. He virtually snubbed him yesterday afternoon."

"Did you know that James Underhill was in the habit of eating peppermints?" Witherspoon asked.

"Everyone knew it, Inspector. He was continually popping those wretched things in his mouth. He never offered them to others, either."

"Did he eat any when you were out in the garden before tea?"

"I'm not sure," she said, her expression thoughtful as she cast her mind back. Finally, she shook her head. "I don't know. Frankly, I was too busy being a proper hostess to Mr. and Mrs. Modean to pay much attention to James."

"If you weren't watchin' him, ma'am," Barnes asked softly, "how can you be so certain he didn't become engaged to your sister?"

She cast the constable a glance that would wither apples. "It's a perfectly reasonable question, Mrs. Grant," the inspector said defensively.

"It's not at all reasonable," she argued. "I wasn't paying much attention to him, but Helen was sitting right next to Mrs. Modean and I most assuredly was paying attention to her. The woman was my guest."

"Couldn't Miss Collier and Mr. Underhill have slipped off for a few moments without your realizing it?" Witherspoon persisted. He'd no idea why he was pressing this particular point so hard, but for some odd reason, he was compelled to find out if Helen Collier's engagement was a figment of her imagination or a reality. It might have some connection to why someone had killed Underhill.

"I suppose so, Inspector," she admitted, "but I don't think it's likely."

"But you don't know for sure that it's impossible," he pressed.

"Of course not, Inspector. As I said, Helen is a grown woman, not a two-year-old. I don't watch her every moment of the day. However, my sister came out to the gardens a few moments after I'd taken Mrs. Modean out there to enjoy the sunshine. That was about five past four in the afternoon. James Underhill arrived with Arthur a few minutes after that. As far as I recall, Helen didn't get up from her chair until we came into the house for tea. So unless she and James discussed and agreed to marry in the few moments between my escorting Mrs. Modean out of the drawing room and Helen's arrival out in the garden, I don't see how this proposal could have taken place."

"But Miss Collier says she came inside before the rest of you," Witherspoon said. "She had a headache. She also said that Underhill escorted her to the bottom of the front staircase and that it was during this time that they finished making their plans to marry."

Chapter 5

Despite the directions she'd been given at the cafe, it took Betsy half the afternoon to find what she hoped was the right street. Morante, apparently, didn't much care that none of his friends appeared to know his exact address.

Taking a deep breath, Betsy stepped off the pavement and onto busy Dean Street. Nimbly dodging a whitechapel cart, she ignored the shouts of the driver and plunged straight toward the entrance to the alley. Gaining the other side, she stopped and peered down the narrow, dark lane. A shiver climbed her spine as she read the small sign attached to the side of the building. Adders Row. Shaking her head, she wondered why an artist, someone who captured beauty, would have a studio in such an ugly, mean-looking place. She supposed it must be because it was cheaper to live here than in most other places in the city.

She headed in, her gaze darting quickly along the row of tiny, derelict houses looking for the one with the "henna-colored window sills." The fellow at the cafe, the one who'd given her the directions to Morante's studio, hadn't had a proper house number. Betsy only hoped sending her along to this nasty little street wasn't his bohemian idea of a good joke. He'd gotten a lot less friendly when she'd told him flat out she wasn't interested in posing for him.

But then she saw the house. It was halfway down the alley, propped against its neighbor like a drunken sailor. The once-white paint was a dull gray, the brickwork along the tiny footpath leading to the front door was crumbling and the windows were covered with a thick layer of grime.

Except the ones on the top floor. Betsy noticed they were sparkling clean. And they had bright henna-colored sills. Taking another fortifying breath, Betsy went up the walk, made a fist and banged on the door.

Nothing.

She pounded again and then plastered her ear to the wood listening for the sound of movement.

"He's gone, dearie."

Startled, Betsy leapt back so fast she stumbled, righted herself and then whirled around to see who'd spoken. Shocked, she gasped and was instantly ashamed of herself. A woman, practically bald, old and pink-eyed like an albino, stood grinning at her. She was bent almost to her waist from age. One gnarled hand clasped a heavy walking stick. "Scared ya, did I? There's no use yer knockin' anymore. He's gone."

"Who?" Betsy asked. She knew who she'd been seeking, but she'd found in the past that pretending to be a bit stupid frequently got a lot of information out of people.

"Whoever it is yer lookin' for," the woman cackled. She moved her stick forward a few inches and followed that action with a tiny step.

"What makes you think I'm lookin' for anyone? Maybe I was just lost," Betsy said.

The old woman shook her head, dislodging the motley shawl from her shoulders and sending it skittering onto the dirty cobblestones. "If ya was lost you'da stayed out there" — she pointed toward Dean Street — "and asked one of them peelers for directions. He not pay ya, then? You wouldn't be the first to come round lookin' for what she's owed and I don't reckon you'll be the last."

Betsy decided to try another tactic. "That's right." She deliberately shifted her accent back to the one she'd been born with, the one she'd worked so hard to lose. " 'E's not paid me a bloomin' bob and I'm tired of waitin' for 'im. You know where 'e's gone?" She jerked her head at the house and put her hands on her hips.

The woman cocked her head to one side and examined Betsy speculatively, her gaze taking in the clean wool jacket and neat broadcloth dress. "Come here." She motioned her toward her, keeping her gaze lowered to Betsy's feet as she walked over to the old woman. "Don't look to me like you're hurtin'," the woman mumbled.

"Them shoes cost a pretty bob or two."

Unable to stop herself, Betsy glanced at the woman's feet. She grimaced in disgust. They'd once been a sturdy pair of proper black walking shoes. But now they were old, scruffed and badly cracked. The sole of the right shoe was tied with a piece of dirty string to keep it attached to a cracked leather upper. She bit her lip, wondering how much money she had with her. Too bad she hadn't taken the time to count it properly. Instead she'd just snatched it out of her top drawer in her hurry to get out of the house unnoticed. She silently debated with herself for a moment and then glanced up at the afternoon sky. The day was gray and overcast, though it was still mid-afternoon; the dark would come quickly. Now though, it was still light and Betsy needed information. She wasn't *that* far from home. She could always take an omnibus. "I'm not 'urtin'," she said, "but I want what's mine. I worked for it." She smiled slyly at the old woman. "I tell ya what, ya look like ya could use a bit o' coin. If ya tell me where 'e's gone, I'll make it worth yer time."

"How much?"

" 'Ow much ya want?" Betsy shot back.

"No reason to give me coin," the woman said thoughtfully.

Betsy's spirits soared.

"He'll only take it off me afore I kin spend it," she mumbled. "Likes his drink, he does, and me daughter's bringin' by a meat pie for me supper, so I don't need no food." She glanced down at Betsy's feet again and then raised her chin, her face split in another toothless grin. "So I don't really need yer coin, but I sure could use me a pair of decent shoes."

The Dirty Duck public house was dark, dank and very much in keeping with its name. Filthy if one bothered to look. Not that seeing the grime was all that easy, Smythe thought, as he stepped into the public bar. The place was too dark to see much of anything at all. Even in the middle of the afternoon. Smythe didn't consider himself all that picky. He'd lived rough plenty when he was a young man out in Australia, but he'd only set foot in this place for one reason. Luckily, that reason was sitting as big as life smack in front of the poxy little fireplace to one side of the bar.

Smythe made his way across the wooden floor, his feet crunching on the sawdust as he walked toward the table where one man sat alone, a tankard in front of him. The air was musty with the scent of stale beer, cheap gin and unwashed bodies.

"Afternoon, Smythe." Blimpey Groggins smiled amiably and motioned at the empty bench on the other side of the rough hewn table. "Have a seat. Ain't seen you in a while."

Smythe looked at the barman. "Two more over 'ere, please," he called and then sat down at the publican's nod. "Afternoon Blimpey. Don't mind if I buy ya a pint, do ya?"

Blimpey laughed. A round-cheeked fellow with ginger-colored hair, he wore an old, dirty porkpie hat and a ready smile. His brown-and-white checked jacket was topped by a bright red scarf tossed jauntily over his shoulder. "I'm not one to look a gift 'orse in the mouth, son. Ya know that. So, how ya been keepin'?"

"Same as always," Smythe replied, digging some coins out of his pocket as the barman brought them their beer. "Ta," he said and handed over the money. He waited till the man left then reached for his glass. "To yer 'ealth, Blimpey."

"I'll drink to that." Blimpey raised his glass and tossed back a mouthful. But he kept his eyes on the coachman. Lowering his glass, he said, "What da ya need, son?"

Smythe grinned. "That's one of the things I like about ya, Blimp, ya get right down to business."

"It's what makes the world go round," Blimpey replied. "Now, what do you want this time?"

Smythe winced inwardly. One part of him felt downright guilty about this, but another part of him, the practical part, didn't see a blooming thing wrong with using his money to do what was right. It wasn't that he couldn't find out information about this case all on his own — he could and would. But using Blimpey's considerable resources was faster and, if he were honest, easier. Besides, if he could help an old friend out with a few extra bob, where was the harm? "Same as always," he replied.

Blimpey Groggins bought and sold information. He'd once been a thief and a pickpocket. But he'd discovered he could make far more money selling knowledge. As he'd been born with a phenomenal memory and a genuine fear of incarceration or even worse, transport to Australia, he'd changed his occupation when he'd almost been caught helping himself to a few pounds he'd found lying about in a silversmith's till.

Blimpey took another swig. "Figured that when you walked in here. What kind ya need this time?"

"Just some general bits and pieces for right now," Smythe said. "Fellow was poisoned — name was James Underhill. I want ya to find out what ya can about 'im," Smythe began.

Blimpey raised his eyebrows. "Underhill's dead?"

"Ya know 'im?"

Blimpey shrugged. "Course not, but I've heard the name." He stroked his chin, his expression thoughtful. "Can't remember where, but I know I've heard it a time or two."

Smythe reconsidered. Blimpey having heard of the dead man cast the victim in a whole new light. "In that case, I'll need to know all ya can find out and I'll need it right quick. 'E's supposed to be some kind of art broker or some such thing —"

"Art!" Blimpey slapped the top of the table. "That's it, then. That's where I've heard of Underhill. His name come up when Jiggers tried to fence some paintings from a toss over in Mayfair."

"Cor blimey, Blimpey, 'ave a care what ya say to me. I do work for a peeler," Smythe warned. "As much as I appreciate yer ways of doin' business, I'd just as soon not know the details of any out and out . . . bloomin' Ada, you know what I mean."

"Don't get yer shirt in a twist, mate," Blimpey replied. "Sometimes I forget who ya works for. How is the inspector?"

" 'E's fine. Now go on with what you were sayin'," Smythe ordered. "What about Underhill?"

"Let me think how to say it now." He grinned wickedly. "All right, then. Let's say a friend of mine was tryin' to sell some lovely paintin's that had come into his possession. Imagine his surprise when he found out they wasn't what he thought they was. Instead of bein' some very valuable pictures what were done by some famous Italians a couple a hundred years ago, they was nothin' but forgeries. Well, my friend, who'd gone to a great deal of trouble to acquire these wonderful works of art, was right narked about them bein' nothin' more than copies and so 'e did a bit of checkin'." Blimpey picked up his drink and took a quick sip. "Seems this weren't the first time somethin' like this had happened.

After a bit more checkin', the name of Underhill cropped up."

Smythe frowned. "You mean this thief was narked because he'd stolen forgeries?"

Blimpey nodded. "Narked enough to dig about and see what's what. That's when Underhill's name come up. But as I remember it, no one could really find out all that much. I mean, let's face it, Smythe, who ya gonna complain to? The police?" He laughed heartily at his own joke.

"I see what ya mean," Smythe muttered.

"I'll see what more I can find out about the fellow," Blimpey said easily. "Anything else ya need?"

"Quite a bit," Smythe said. He didn't completely understand whether Underhill was supposed to be a forger or a thief but decided it would be better to let Blimpey sniff about a bit before he worried about it anymore.

"Good. Nice to know I can count on you to give me a bit of business." Blimpey finished off his drink and looked pointedly at his empty glass. "If we're goin' to be here awhile, I could use another round."

"Order us another," Smythe said, "because there's a lot I've got to tell ya yet."

"It's goin' to be complicated, is it?" Blimpey waved at the publican. "Complicated costs."

"Don't worry about the lolly," Smythe replied. "I'm good for it."

"I wasn't questionin' that," Blimpey assured

him. "I was just wonderin' how fast you're goin' to be wantin' some answers. I might have to put one of me boys on it and that'll cost a bit more, that's all."

"Put whoever ya need to on it." Smythe waved a hand dismissively. " 'Cause I want answers quick and there's a whole bunch of people I need to know about."

"Which one of them do you believe, Inspector?" Barnes asked softly.

"I'm not sure," Witherspoon replied. He kept his eye on the closed drawing room door, not wanting either Miss Collier or Mrs. Grant to pop in while he and the constable were trying to decide which one of them was a liar. "What do either of them have to gain by lying? That's the question, Barnes." He sighed. "But, of course, at this point in the investigation, it's too soon to answer that question."

"Well, you can have another go at Miss Collier," Barnes said. "Why did you want to question her again?"

"Because she was so hysterical this afternoon, I wasn't able to get a complete statement out of her." He frowned anxiously. "I do so hope she's calmed down a bit."

"We'll know in a moment," Barnes whispered as footsteps sounded in the hallway.

Helen Collier swept into the drawing room. Her face was swollen from weeping, she carried a crumpled handkerchief in her hand and her mouth trembled as she struggled to hold back her tears.

Witherspoon cringed. Drat. She didn't look in the least calmed. Perhaps speaking to her now wasn't such a good idea after all. "I'm sorry for your loss, ma'am," he said gently, "but, as I'm sure you realize, there are a few questions I neglected to ask when we spoke earlier today. But perhaps it would be best if I came back another time. Tomorrow, perhaps?"

"No, Inspector." She wiped her eyes and lifted her chin. "That won't be necessary. I want to help. I'll do whatever I can to bring James's killer to justice. Ask me anything you like." She took a deep breath, straightened her spine and then walked over to the settee. Sitting down, she folded her hands in her lap and looked up at him expectantly.

For a moment, the inspector couldn't think of one single thing to ask.

It was the constable who came to his rescue. "Could you tell us if you know of anyone who disliked your . . . uh . . . fiancé?"

Grateful, Witherspoon nodded at Barnes and then focused his attention on Helen Collier. It wouldn't do to be swayed too much by pity. But she was either genuinely distressed by the man's death or one of the best actresses in the world. In the past few years he'd learned to be a bit careful of believing in appearances. Gracious, he'd seen murderers weep and wail over the corpses of their victims and then turn right around and do it again. Not that he thought everyone was prone to such behaviour. Oh no, but he'd learned to be cautious in his judgments. Miss Collier might appear to be most distraught, but that didn't mean she could be eliminated as a suspect.

"Disliked him? You mean socially?"

"Did he have any enemies?" the inspector clarified.

"James had no enemies," she declared.

"None?"

"None, Inspector," she replied. "I've no idea why anyone would want to kill him. He was a gentleman."

"Your sister insists that your relationship with Mr. Underhill was a business — not a social — relationship."

"Must we go over this again?" Helen sighed wearily. "That is how we first met. James took care of selling my father's art collection when he passed away. I'll admit that Mary dealt with him more than I did. But the relationship wasn't merely business, despite what my sister would have you believe. For God's sake, he's escorted the both of us to galleries and museums. He's been here a dozen times for dinner or tea. I don't know why Mary keeps insisting it was only a business relationship. That's simply not true. We stopped at his country house a few weeks back on our way back from the north. I don't understand it."

"It's quite natural for people to try and distance themselves from murder victims," Witherspoon said softly. "Did you know that your sister wouldn't approve of your engagement to Underhill?"

"It made no difference whether Mary approved or not," Helen declared. "I live in this house, Inspector, because it's convenient. But I've my own money. Papa made sure of that."

Witherspoon tried to keep from looking as surprised as he felt. Mary Grant had specifically claimed that her sister lived here because she had no money. Now Helen was saying just the opposite. But which of them was telling the truth? As he'd have to do some more digging to know the answer to this query, he decided to try another tactic. "Could you tell us what happened yesterday afternoon?"

"I've already made a statement."

The inspector didn't want to remind her that she'd been so hysterical she'd not made any sense. "We'd like you to go over it again," he said tactfully. "There might be a detail or two that you can recall now."

"The Modeans had been invited to tea." She shrugged. "Neville wanted to sell his three Caldararo paintings to Mr. Modean. They were going to make the final arrangements yesterday afternoon."

"So you went out into the garden when the Modeans arrived?" he persisted, hoping to get her to speak freely.

"No, Mary took Mrs. Modean into the garden," she replied calmly. "Mr. Modean went into the study with Neville. I went out into the garden a few minutes after Mary and Mrs. Modean and then James and Arthur came out."

"Why didn't you go out with your sister and Mrs. Modean?" Witherspoon asked.

"Because I wanted to wait and have a private word with James," Helen replied. "I knew James had been invited, you see. But Arthur met him at the front door and took him straight into the drawing room. As I didn't wish to be rude, I went on outside. We'd been out there enjoying the fresh air for about ten minutes when Arthur and James came out. It was rather awkward. Mary wasn't all that pleased to see James and she didn't bother to hide it."

"She was rude to him?"

"Hardly, Inspector. My sister is never blatantly rude. She was merely cold, distant." Helen's eyes flashed with resentment. "She ordered him about like he was a common servant. James was far too much a gentleman to make a scene, so he did what she asked and got that upstart American a chair. Not that the man appreciated it. He virtually snubbed him."

"Snubbed him? How?" Witherspoon pressed. This was getting quite interesting.

"Oh, you know." Helen shifted, her eyes narrowed angrily. "It wasn't anything he actually said, it was the way he barely acknowledged James. For a moment, I was afraid he wasn't even going to speak to James."

The inspector tucked that bit of knowledge

into the back of his mind. Americans were generally quite friendly. But he had other questions to ask, other ideas that needed checking. "Did you see Mr. Underhill take out his tin of peppermints?"

She hesitated for a moment, her expression thoughtful. "It's difficult, Inspector. James did love his mints. He always had a tin or two in his pocket. I honestly can't remember whether I saw him take them out or whether I was just so used to seeing him with them that I'm imagining I did." Her forehead wrinkled in concentration. "He took the tin out and ate one. I remember because it was right when Mary asked him to get Mr. Modean a chair . . . that's right. He put the tin down on the table."

Barnes looked up from his notebook. "Why didn't he put it in his pocket?"

The Inspector nodded approvingly. Excellent question. Obviously his methods were beginning to wear off on his constable. "Yes, why didn't he?"

"I've no idea, Inspector. But I remember the entire sequence of events now. James had just put a mint in his mouth when Mary asked him to get a chair for Mr. Modean. Of course, as he's a gentleman, he complied with her request immediately and instead of putting the tin back in his inside coat pocket . . ."

Witherspoon interrupted. "His overcoat?"

"That's where he generally carried them," she replied. "But as I was saying, he simply laid them down on the table and went over to the terrace. Yes, that's right, because I was going to remind him not to forget them when we went inside for tea." Her voice faltered and her eyes filled with tears. To give her her due, she took a deep breath and straightened her spine. "But of course, I didn't. I quite forgot all about the mints."

"You're sure the tin was still on the table when you left?" Barnes asked.

"Absolutely."

Witherspoon asked, "Did Mr. Underhill offer them to the rest of you?"

Helen smiled uneasily, as though she were a bit embarrassed. "Well, no, not exactly. I know it sounds silly, Inspector, but everyone is entitled to one fault. James was just a bit selfish with his mints. So, no, he didn't offer them around. He never did."

Witherspoon glanced at Barnes and saw by the knowing expression on the constable's face that he grasped the significance of what Helen Collier had just told them.

"Did you see how many mints were in the tin when he opened it?" Witherspoon asked.

Helen considered the question. "No, I can't say that I did. Is it important?"

The inspector wasn't sure. It could be. Unfortunately, there wasn't any way to really know. It was very possible that the mints had been poisoned while they were out on the table, or considering what Helen had told them about his habit of not offering them to others, they could have been poisoned at any time with the killer banking on the fact that Underhill never shared them with others. Drat. "It could be very important, Miss Collier. Er, this is a rather delicate question. You told us earlier that you and Mr. Underhill agreed to become engaged when you came into the house a few moments before tea. Is that correct?"

"Yes," she said. "I told the others I had a headache from the sun and needed to lie down. But that was just an excuse for James and I to have a few moments of privacy. He escorted me inside and proposed to me. It wasn't unexpected, Inspector," she explained dryly. "When you get to be my age, you don't play the simpering miss. He proposed at the foot of the staircase and I accepted. I then went upstairs to check on my appearance. We were going to announce the engagement at tea and I wanted to look my best."

"When you say it wasn't unexpected . . ." Witherspoon hesitated. This was decidedly an awkward question. "What, precisely, led you to believe Mr. Underhill was going to propose? Had he mentioned it to you?"

Helen crossed her arms over her chest. "I fail to see how that's any of your concern."

Witherspoon sighed inwardly. "Ma'am, I assure you, under any other circumstances it wouldn't be the concern of the police. However, your fiancé was poisoned."

"Well, I didn't do it," she snapped.

"We're not implying you did, ma'am," he said hastily. "We're merely trying to learn as much as we can about everything that happened yesterday. There appears to be some question as to whether or not your engagement was real —"

"Of course it was real," she interrupted. "If you must know, he asked me yesterday morning."

"Mr. Underhill was here yesterday morning?" Witherspoon exclaimed. Egads, why hadn't someone mentioned that before?

"No, he wasn't," she corrected. "I went to see him."

"You went to his house?" the inspector asked.

"To his rooms, yes." She glanced down at the carpet and then lifted her chin defiantly. "James doesn't have a house here in town. He has lodgings in a private home in Bayswater. It's not that he can't afford a home — he most certainly can. I mean, he could. But there wouldn't be any point to it, surely. After we'd married, we were going to move to his cottage out in the country, so there wasn't any reason for him to go to the trouble and expense of finding a house here in town."

"Yes, yes, of course," Witherspoon said quickly. "I quite understand." He was amazed that rather than the woman being embarrassed about admitting she went to a gentleman's rooms alone, she appeared to be mortified because the man she'd consented to wed lived in lodgings. "And he asked you to marry him then? What time was this?"

"It was early, just after eight in the morning. I went out right after breakfast."

"Did his landlady see you?" Barnes asked.

"No, James was just leaving when I arrived. He was in a hurry for a business appointment. He proposed to me right then, I accepted and then we caught a hansom."

"Together?"

"No, separately. I came home. James went on about his business."

"Did he say where he was going?" Witherspoon asked.

"As a matter of fact, he did," she said proudly. "He was going to Soho. There was some artist or other he wanted to see."

Mrs. Jeffries stood on the south side of the Thames Embankment staring at the Houses of Parliament across the river. Traffic on the river moved briskly, barges and flat boats, some of them so loaded with goods they rode low in the water, chugged and skimmed alongside steamers and ferries belching black smoke into the gray afternoon. Every few seconds, she cast her gaze over her shoulder, watching for her prey. She spotted him coming out of St. Thomas's Hospital.

"Good day, Doctor," she called gaily, waving her umbrella to get his attention.

Preoccupied, he looked around vaguely and then his face broke into a huge grin when he saw her. "Good day, Mrs. Jeffries," he said, hurrying toward her. "I've been expecting you."

"Of course you were," she agreed with a chuckle. They were old collaborators. Dr. Bosworth frequently advised her on the inspector's homicides. He had a way of looking at corpses that frequently shed light on the hows, whys and wherefores of the crime itself. Most of his medical colleagues didn't share some of his rather radical views about what one could and couldn't learn from a dead body, but that made no difference to the good doctor. Except when he was helping Mrs. Jeffries, he kept his observations quiet around others in the medical establishment. Perhaps when he was very old and ready to retire, he'd publish the notebooks he kept on his work.

"I'm afraid I don't have much time this afternoon," he said apologetically as he took her arm. "I've an appointment at the medical school in fifteen minutes. Perhaps you'd care to walk with me? It's just down there." He pointed to the buildings at the other end of the hospital.

"You know why I've come," she said.

"James Underhill," he replied. "Poisoned. Cyanide in the peppermints. They were impregnated with the stuff."

"Impregnated how?"

He steered her around a lollygagging group of young men, medical students by the look of them, and in no hurry to reach their destination. "I'm not sure. I suspect the poison was, however it was obtained, soaked in a small amount of water and then the water dropped onto the individual mints. There wasn't much left to analyze, only the inside wrapping paper and a few granules."

"Are you absolutely certain the poison was in the mints and not something else?" she asked. It was essential to clarify how the victim had ingested the lethal dose.

Amused by the question, Bosworth smiled. "Mrs. Jeffries, take my word for it. It was the mints. Cyanide kills so quickly that if he'd ingested it any other way, he'd have dropped dead before he had that last mint."

She felt a bit foolish. "You're right, of course. Silly of me to ask."

"Not at all," he said gallantly. "Perfectly reasonable question."

They'd reached their destination. Mrs. Jeffries glanced at the groups of students cluttered along the walkway leading to the front door of the medical school. Dressed for the most part in thick black overcoats and stiff collared white shirts, they all looked much alike. "You're very kind, Doctor," she murmured. "Look at all of them." She swept her hand at a knot of students huddled at the far end of the building. "All male. What a pity. There's no reason at all a woman couldn't be a physican or a surgeon."

"I agree," Bosworth replied with a grin. "Several of them are. It's fairly rare, though, and they meet with a lot of resistance."

She clucked her tongue in disgust. "One day,

perhaps even in my lifetime, women will march up to this building and take their rightful place."

"If it's any comfort to you," Bosworth said, "not every country is as rigid about educating women as Britain. In Pennsylvania they actually have a medical college to train women doctors. I must be off, Mrs. Jeffries. Is there anything else you needed to ask me?"

"No, but do let me know if you think of anything that might be helpful."

"Right." He turned toward the building then whirled back around. "I really would like you to meet an American colleague of mine who's in town for a few days . . ." He paused, not quite sure how to tell her about having had to invite the inspector.

"Is it the person who Inspector Witherspoon said you wanted him to meet?" she asked sweetly.

"Yes, but I only said that because your Wiggins ran into me in your neighborhood last evening — I was on my way to see you, but I could hardly tell that to your employer, so I said I was coming to see him. But the point is" — Bosworth blushed a fiery red — "I'd really like you to meet this man. He's quite an expert on pathology . . . he's a number of ideas about what the dead can tell us."

Heads swiveled at Bosworth's words. But he ignored the odd stares cast his way. "I'll send you a note," he called to Mrs. Jeffries as he turned and hurried into the building.

135

He was gone before she had a chance to say goodbye.

Betsy's feet were freezing. She got out of the hansom at the junction of Addison Crescent and Holland Park Road. Wincing, as the pavement was cold, she told herself she'd not far to walk. But she hadn't dared take the hansom all the way home. Wiggins or Smythe or Mrs. Goodge or *someone* would have seen and started asking why she was using a cab when it wasn't even dark out.

But it had been worth it. Betsy flinched as her stockinged feet hit a rough spot on the uneven pavement. These stockings would never be the same, that was for sure. But the loss of a pair of shoes and stockings was nothing compared to what she'd gained.

Betsy nodded at a maid sweeping the front door stoop of a house she hurried past. She hunkered down slightly, hoping the girl wouldn't notice her feet. The less said about it the better. There were some, she thought, that would get right nasty about what she'd done. One in particular who would have a fit if he knew she'd been traipsing about London like this. She quickened her pace, glad the day was overcast and that there weren't many people out. Luckily, her dress was on the longish side, so she reckoned she could make it into the house and up to her room without running into any of her friends.

Betsy breathed a sigh of relief as she turned the corner and saw that the road leading to the inspector's house was clear. "Ow," she yelped as a sharp pain lanced straight into her right heel. She yanked her foot up, which caused her to lurch to one side. "Ow, ow, ow," she mumbled, trying to regain her balance without actually having to put her foot back down. She managed to steady herself by grabbing onto the wrought iron fence of the house a few doors down from the inspector's. Leaning over, she dug a pebble out of her flesh, gave it a good glare and tossed it onto the road.

"Betsy? What's goin' on 'ere?"

The familiar voice rattled her to the quick. Betsy whirled around, forgetting that one of her feet was still a good two inches off the ground. She stumbled heavily to one side. Smythe lunged for her, catching her before she completely crumbled.

"Bloomin' Ada," he cried, "what's 'appened? Are you all right?"

"I'm fine." She struggled to regain her footing, but he kept a tight grip on her waist.

"Ya don't look fine," he accused, frightened that she was ill. He examined her closely, his gaze starting at the top of her head and moving slowly down her slender figure. "Cor blimey," he yelled, "where in the ruddy blue blazes is yer shoe?"

Betsy tried to think of how to answer. "Well, it's a bit complicated."

He reached over and tugged the hem of her dress up. "Where's the other one? Betsy, you've no shoes on!"

"Yes, I know that," she replied.

"What in the blazes is ya doin' out 'ere without yer shoes?" he demanded. "It's not the dead of winter, but it ain't 'igh summer either. Now you just wait 'ere and I'll nip along to the 'ouse and fetch 'em for ya."

"They're not in the house," she admitted.

He studied her for a moment and then his eyes narrowed. "Then where are they?"

"Well . . ." She hesitated. "If you really must know, they're in Soho. I gave them to an old lady in exchange for information."

Chapter 6

"Would you care for a glass of sherry before dinner, sir?" Mrs. Jeffries asked the inspector as soon as he'd taken off his coat and hat. "Mrs. Goodge said it'll be a few minutes yet."

She wanted to find out what he'd learned before he sat down to eat. Sometimes, she'd noticed, he tended to get a bit drowsy on a full stomach.

"A lovely idea," he said, heading for the drawing room. He plopped down in his favorite chair while Mrs. Jeffries poured them both a glass of Harveys. The custom of sharing a glass of sherry with his housekeeper helped him to relax after a day's work. From the inspector's point of view, it was absolutely necessary. Talking about the case did so help him to clarify matters in his own mind. Sometimes he wondered how he'd actually solved so many murders, but as Mrs. Jeffries frequently pointed out when he began to doubt his abilities, he'd been born with an "instinct" or "inner voice" when it came to catching murderers. But inner voice or not, it really did help to have someone to talk with.

"How did your investigation go today?" she asked cheerfully.

"Very well," he allowed. Then he admitted, "Actually, I don't know if I learned anything important or not. As you know, this early in an investigation I tend to get a bit muddled, but I'm sure I'll make sense of it eventually."

"You always do, sir," she assured him. Gracious, she was going to have to dig it out of him tonight. "Did you go back to the Grant house?"

"Oh, yes," he said, taking a quick sip. "I got full statements from everyone, even the servants. Mind you, Mr. and Mrs. Modean weren't there." He frowned. "They weren't at the hotel either, but Constable Barnes and I shall have another go at seeing them tomorrow morning. We intend to get there quite early, before they go out for the day."

"They haven't left the hotel?" she asked.

"No, no. We've a man on duty there. The manager would let us know if they'd tried to check out. They were merely out when I went there, that's all."

"Do you expect them to be able to shed any light on this matter?"

"I'm not sure," he replied. "On the surface it would appear that they simply had the misfortune to be in the wrong drawing room at the wrong time. But after what I found out today, I'm not so sure that's the case."

"Indeed? I take it, then, you were able to learn something useful, sir?"

"I do think so, Mrs. Jeffries." He put his glass down on the table next to him and, leaning forward slightly, told her every little detail about the interviews with everyone from the Grant household.

Mrs. Jeffries was a skillful listener. It was one of her greatest talents. She never interrupted and never asked questions before he'd finished speaking. By the time he'd completed his narrative, her own mental list of questions was at the ready. She fired her first shot. "So the tin was out in the garden for at least ten minutes," she said. "Anyone could have tampered with it."

"True." He pursed his lips. "But I'm not so sure it would be as easy as it sounds. According to the kitchen staff, none of the guests went back to the garden after they'd all come inside."

"Meaning that none of them would have had the opportunity to poison the mints," she said slowly. "But surely there's more than one way out to the garden."

"There is a side door," he acknowledged, "but it was locked tight and no one seems to know where the key is."

Her mind whirled at the possibilities. "I see," she replied thoughtfully. "Is it your opinion, then, that the mints were tampered with while they were still in Mr. Underhill's possession?"

"What do you mean?"

"Do you think someone waited till he'd set them on the table and then added the poison, or was the deed done some other way?" she suggested. "Perhaps the tin was switched when the victim wasn't aware of it?"

Witherspoon pondered the idea for a moment and sighed. "Frankly, Mrs. Jeffries, I don't know. I suppose it could have happened either way. We simply don't have enough information yet. The servants insist none of the guests went back out to the garden and the side door was locked."

"Which means that for someone to have tampered with the mints while they were outside, the staff would have had to be lying or not noticed one of the guests going out. Or, the killer would have had a key to the side door."

"That's right." Witherspoon took another sip of sherry. "And I don't think the servants are lying. Why should they? They've nothing to gain by keeping quiet. The staff was preparing a high tea, Mrs. Jeffries. There were half a dozen of them working. Scullery maids, a cook, the butler, a footman. I simply can't believe all of them would lie about whether or not one of the guests had trotted back out to the garden."

"What about the key, sir?" she pressed.

"There isn't one," he said. "I mean, there was one, but apparently, it's been lost for years."

She got up and reached for his empty glass. "Another one, sir?" At his nod, she walked slowly to the sideboard and the bottle of sherry. "Did you have a look at the lock, sir?"

"Oh yes, Mrs. Jeffries. It's old and rusty looking. I don't believe that door has been opened in years." He shrugged. "I'm afraid this case is going to be quite complex. Quite complex, indeed."

"They always are, sir." She smiled reassuringly. "And you always solve them."

Luty and Hatchet arrived just as they finished cleaning up the kitchen. Betsy put the last of the supper dishes in the cupboard, dusted her hands off and, ignoring Smythe's glinty-eyed look of disapproval, took her usual place with the others at the kitchen table. Obviously, he was still upset over their argument earlier that afternoon. To put it mildly, they'd had words.

"I'm so glad you and Luty got here early," Mrs. Jeffries said. "We've a lot to talk about this evening."

"Good thing I had the kettle on the boil," Mrs. Goodge said, setting the brown teapot down and then taking her own seat. "We'll need a cuppa or two by the time we're all done here. I've got a might lot to say tonight."

"What did you git out of the inspector?" Luty asked eagerly.

"Quite a bit." Mrs. Jeffries smiled. "But I think before I tell you what he found out, we ought to see what everyone else has learned."

" 'Ow come?" Wiggins demanded. "Usually we 'ear the inspector's bits first." He wasn't all that keen to report on the day's activities. He'd not learned a blooming thing.

"Actually, the inspector's made rather good progress," she announced. "Who wants to go first?"

"I didn't hear much today," Smythe said. "But I've got me feelers out and I should 'ave somethin' tomorrow."

"I found out that Neville Grant's not near as rich as you'd think," Luty said proudly. "That's why he's sellin' his paintings to Tyrell Modean. He needs the cash."

"How badly?" Smythe inquired.

"Bad enough to sell them Caldararos," Luty replied seriously. "And he loves them more than just about anythin'. He wanted 'em bad enough to marry just so's he could git his hands on 'em."

"Disgusting, isn't it?" Mrs. Goodge put in. "That's what I found out today as well. That's the only reason he married the poor woman. She owned those paintings and he wanted them. They were her dowry."

"Why'd she want to marry 'im?" Wiggins asked. " 'E's old as the hills and not very nice."

"Because she was sick and tired of bein' an old maid," Mrs. Goodge said bluntly. "She and her sister spent most of their life taking care of their father. About ten years ago, old Mr. Collier finally died. But the estate they lived on was entailed so it went to some distant cousin. All Mary and Helen got was their father's art collection. Helen put hers in a bank vault. Mary gave hers to Neville Grant in return for a proposal of marriage."

"Cor blimey, that's right cold-blooded." Smythe made a face. He couldn't imagine spending his life with someone he didn't truly care about. "Was Neville Grant the best the poor woman could do?"

"Yes," Luty replied. "For a woman of her class and background, I expect he was the best she could hope for. She's fifty-five if she's a day. Ten years ago she'd have been pushin' forty-five. When you git to be that old, there ain't much for a woman to choose from. Most of the men of her own age are already hitched. If they ain't and they got money, they could git 'em a young woman." She snorted derisively. "Course it seems to me if she'd had any sense she'd a sold them paintin's and taken off for some fun and adventure."

"I suspect," Hatchet said smoothly, "that Mrs. Grant may have had a number of reasons for wanting to wed Mr. Grant."

"What reasons?" Luty asked indignantly. "He's mean, he's ugly and he ain't rich."

"But perhaps he was less mean, less ugly and a good deal richer ten years ago." Hatchet smiled slyly.

Luty eyed him suspiciously, wondering what he knew. "And just what do you mean by that?"

Hatchet smiled benignly. "All in good time, madam. All in good time."

"How bad is Grant's financial position?" Mrs. Jeffries asked.

"About as bad as it kin git," Luty said. "He owes just about everyone. The butcher, the baker, the bank, his wife's dressmaker. Everyone. Some of 'em are startin' to press him pretty hard for what they're owed too. Sellin' those Caldararos to Modean came just in the nick of time. Otherwise, he'd probably be losin' his house. Seems most of Grant's investments have gone sour in the last few years. He's been livin' on borrowed money to keep up that fancy house and all them servants."

"The whole town knows about it too," Mrs. Goodge added eagerly. "It's common gossip. But the Grants, Mrs. Grant in particular, has expensive taste and they've been livin' above their means for years. Guess it finally caught up with them. According to what I heard, they're so hard up for money that Mrs. Grant was pressing her sister to sell her art collection as well."

"Maybe that's why she was so set against Helen Collier's engagement to Underhill," Mrs. Jeffries mused, remembering the information she'd gotten out of the inspector. "If the marriage took place, she'd never get her hands on those paintings. Oh dear, I'm getting ahead of myself again. Does anyone have anything else to contribute?"

Wiggins cleared his throat. "Like I said, I don't 'ave much to say. With the inspector and the police bein' at the Grant 'ouse today, I couldn't get too close. There might 'ave been a bit of comin' and goin' amongst the servants, but the only one I got near enough to talk to was a shirty little footman who weren't 'alf full of 'imself. But 'e didn't know much. 'E weren't even there when the murder 'appened. Mrs. Grant 'ad sent 'im off

146

on an errand." He gave an embarrassed shrug. "It's not much, but it were the best I could do today."

"Not to worry, lad," Smythe said kindly. "We all 'ave our bad days. I didn't find out much either. But tomorrow'll be better for both of us."

"Right then," Mrs. Jeffries said briskly. "Before I get on to the inspector's bits and pieces, I want to tell you what I learned from Dr. Bosworth." She told them of her meeting that day with the doctor, omitting only that she'd been invited to dinner. Then she charged right in to the rest of what she'd gotten out of their employer.

"I don't quite understand." Hatchet frowned. "Didn't you just tell us that the servants said no one had come through the kitchen?"

"True," she replied. "But there is a side door. It was locked when the inspector tried it, but that doesn't mean it was locked yesterday afternoon. The inspector said he looked at the lock and it didn't appear to have been opened recently, but can one really tell? Even a rusty lock can be opened with the right key."

"I'm gittin' confused," Luty muttered. "The servants didn't see anyone go out to the garden, the key to the side door is missin', Tyrell Modean snubbed Underhill, Mary Grant or Helen Collier is lyin' about whether she was or wasn't engaged to the victim . . . land o' Goshen, this is gittin' too muddled for a body to know whether they're comin' or goin'. Why don't we take this one suspect at a time?"

"I don't think we ought to bother," Mrs. Goodge put in. "We're putting the cart before the horse. We don't know that any of the people at the Grant house when Underhill died really are suspects. We don't know for a fact that the mints were tampered with at the Grant house. They coulda been doctored well before that afternoon."

"That'd be a bit risky," Wiggins muttered.

"Not really. Underhill never shared," the cook insisted. "We just heard that. He was famous for not handin' them mints around. Seems to me the killer must have known this. Them mints coulda been poisoned ages ago. When you think of it, it's a real good way of murderin' someone. All the killer had to do then was wait until Underhill ate the right one."

Nanette Lanier locked the outside door and hurried off toward the intersection, her expression preoccupied. As soon as she'd turned the corner, a figure stepped out of the shadows and crossed over to unlock the door Nanette had so carefully locked.

Moving quickly, he stepped inside and shut the door. The hallway was in total darkness. He stepped onto the bottom stair, wincing when it creaked in the quiet of the night. But there was no choice. None at all. It had to be done.

He took a long, calming breath and climbed to the first floor landing. Pausing there, he scanned the area, making sure that no one was in Nanette's flat. But behind the closed door of her quarters there was nothing but silence.

He continued up the stairs. On the third floor, he stopped and listened, wanting to see if he could hear anyone following him. He still wasn't sure it was safe, even with Underhill dead. But he heard nothing.

He moved to the door. There was a faint light coming from underneath it. But he'd expected that. She slept with the lamp burning now. Taking a key out of his pocket, he gently eased it into the lock, turned it slowly and grasped the handle when he heard the faint click of the mechanism sliding into place. Cautiously, he eased into the room, sticking his head in first to make sure it was empty.

There was no one inside the tiny drawing room. To his left was a small kitchen and on the far side of the room, behind the shabby settee, was the door that led to the bedroom. Without giving himself time to think about what he was doing, he closed the door and tiptoed quietly into the kitchen.

There, on the rickety old table next to the cooker, sat the bottle. He gave it a shake. As expected, it was almost empty. He cast a quick glance at the bedroom door. He didn't want her coming in and catching him.

He put the bottle down and reached into his pocket, taking out another, identical bottle to the one on the table. He put it down and then removed the stoppers from both of them. He poured the contents of the one he'd brought with him into the other, almost empty bottle.

By the time he'd finished his task and returned both bottles to their rightful place, the one on the table now full and the one in his pocket now almost empty, his face was covered in a sheen of sweat.

By the time he made it safely back down the stairs and out into the chilly night, his whole body was drenched.

"I found out something today," Betsy said when they'd finally finished nattering on about the wretched mints. "And I know it's not about the murder, but we are still supposed to be lookin' for Irene Simmons."

"Of course, Betsy," Mrs. Jeffries said cheerfully. "We're all most interested."

"Especially me." Hatchet gave her a wide smile. "As I too have learned something that may shed some light on the young lady's disappearance."

Betsy cleared her throat. "Well, I started thinkin' that maybe we ought to backtrack a bit here."

"Yes, yes, of course, Betsy. How very clever of you," Mrs. Jeffries said. She wished Betsy would get on with it and then immediately felt ashamed of herself. Irene's disappearance was every bit as important as finding Underhill's killer. "Presumably that's why you're trying to track down this Spanish artist. Were your efforts today fruitful?"

"I'm not really sure. But I went to his studio in Soho." Betsy paused and waited. All eyes were on her. She wanted their complete attention for her next revelation. "And I found out he disappeared the same day that Irene did."

"Actually, it was the very same evening," Hatchet added. "And under most unusual circumstances."

Betsy gasped involuntarily. She'd sacrificed a pair of shoes to find out this information and here Hatchet not only knew it, but he'd got the better of her to boot. Well, blow me for a game of tin soldiers, she thought resentfully. She shot Smythe a quick glance and her eyes narrowed angrily as she saw the grin dancing around his mouth. Unable to stop herself, she kicked him under the table.

"Ouch!" Smythe yelped. "Oh, sorry," he said, not wanting to embarrass Betsy even though the minx blooming well deserved it, "got a sudden cramp in me foot. Go on with what you were tellin' us, Hatchet."

Hatchet, to his credit, seemed to realize that he'd stolen Betsy's thunder. "Forgive me, Miss Betsy," he said gallantly, "I interrupted you."

"Ya interrupt me all the time," Luty muttered. "I don't hear ya askin' for my forgiveness."

"Really, madam." Hatchet sniffed disdainfully. "That charge is so uncalled for it does not even merit a response. Now, Miss Betsy, please go on."

"Thank you," Betsy said primly. "Well, as I was saying, I went to Soho and found out that this Gaspar Morante had taken himself off most unexpectedly. And what's more, I wasn't the only one who's been round looking for him, either. Seems that several people have been trying to find him, and one of them was James Underhill."

"Underhill," Mrs. Jeffries said. "Are you sure?"

Betsy nodded. "Oh, yes. He was there on the day he was murdered. That morning. When Morante didn't answer the door, Underhill went round asking the neighbors if they knew where he'd got off to. But no one did, of course. My source says Underhill was right upset too, tried to break into Morante's house but a couple of lads threatened to go get the policeman from over on Dean Street if he didn't leave."

"I'm glad to see your information tallys somewhat with mine," Hatchet began. "I —"

Enjoying her moment in the limelight, Betsy continued eagerly. "Did you find out about Morante? You know, how he was asking questions about Irene Simmons on the night before she disappeared?"

"What kind of questions?" Mrs. Goodge asked.

"He wanted to know where the girl lived," Hatchet put in. He'd restrained himself admirably, or so he thought, but really, he'd something to contribute here as well.

"Right," Betsy agreed. "And then the next day, Morante's gone and she's gone. I think it's a bit more than a coincidence. I think if we can find him, we'll find her."

"If she's still alive," Luty said darkly.

"Thanks for not tattling on me," Betsy said softly as she and Smythe cleared up the last of the tea things. The kitchen was empty save for Fred, who refused to go up even with Wiggins as long as there was a chance a morsel of food might come his way.

"Humph." Smythe snorted faintly. "It's one thing for me to get irritated with you, lass. But I'll not have the others tearin' a strip off ya. Though it were foolish, Betsy, givin' that woman yer shoes."

Betsy smiled. "I've seen you do almost the same."

He bit his tongue to keep from telling her it was different for him. He could afford it. She couldn't. He knew her gesture hadn't just been done to get information out of an old woman. Betsy had done it as much out of pity as anything else. But now the lass hadn't a decent pair of work shoes left. Only her Sunday best and a pair of old ones that he knew had holes in the soles.

Blast it anyway, he thought grimly, he'd money enough to buy her a whole shop full of shoes and he couldn't. Sometimes he despaired of being able to tell her the truth. Or any of the others, for that matter. He was a rich man. He'd come back to England five years ago with a blooming fortune. On a whim, he'd stopped in to see Euphemia, Inspector Witherspoon's late aunt and a dear friend of his. Euphemia, God rest her soul, had known she was dying. She'd willed her house and fortune to her only living relative, the incredibly naive Gerald Witherspoon. She'd begged Smythe to stay on in her home and keep an eye on her nephew. Smythe, under the guise of being a coachman, had agreed. Then Mrs. Jeffries and Betsy had come and everything had changed. Before you could snap your fingers, they were investigating murders and looking out for one another and becoming almost like a family. In the meantime, his fortune had grown like weeds in a flower bed and he was even richer than before. But he couldn't say one word about it — all he could do was secretly help the others when they needed it. If he told them the truth, everything would change. They'd feel differently about him. They wouldn't treat him the same. He wouldn't be one of them. Smythe wouldn't risk that. He wouldn't lose the only family he'd known in years. Most especially, he wouldn't risk losing Betsy. He clenched his hands into fists, frustrated because the woman he cared about would be trotting about London with blooming holes in her shoes. "I've done things like that before," he admitted, "but it isn't always wise."

"Don't go on about it," she said wearily. She didn't regret what she'd done. Well, perhaps just a bit. But she didn't want to talk it to death either. After all, she was the one who'd be wearing her old, worn out shoes till she got her next quarter's salary.

"All right, lass, I'll not say another word." He'd find a way to buy her some new shoes.

"Good." She favored him with one of her wan smiles. "What are you going to be up to tomorrow?" She wished she were working on the murder too. Despite Luty's dark predictions, she had a feeling that Irene Simmons was fine. She didn't know why, but that's how she felt. Not being really involved in the murder investigation was beginning to niggle her a bit. Not much, but a bit.

"Oh, just out and about diggin' up what I can," he replied. "I'm trying to find out more about Underhill's dealings. Seems to me like we don't know much about the bloke. Not even what kind of a 'ouse 'e lives in."

"Wiggins said he'd take a gander at Underhill's lodgings."

"I thought 'e were goin' back to the Grant 'ouse."

"He is," Betsy replied. "But then he's going to have a snoop around Underhill's rooms." She sighed. "It feels a bit strange not being involved like the rest of ya is."

"You're doin' somethin' important," he pointed out. "As we said before, Underhill's dead. This girl might still be alive."

"I know," she replied. "I know it's important.

But it still feels a bit odd. I guess I'll have another go at Soho tomorrow. Talk to a few more artists. This time, though, I'll hang onto my shoes."

"Betsy," he began and then hesitated. "Be careful. I mean, Soho isn't the best area of London."

Betsy laughed. "I'm always careful, Smythe. You know that."

As they'd arranged, Witherspoon met Constable Barnes at the hotel early the next morning. This was most definitely an establishment that catered to the rich.

Settees and balloon-backed chairs, upholstered in rich brown and green leather, were placed comfortably around the huge lobby. Long velvet curtains festooned the windows, dampening the noise from the busy street outside. A long oak-paneled reception area, behind which an army of smartly uniformed young men worked busily, stretched along the length of one wall. Bellmen and housemaids, laden with silver trays and hoisting huge carpet bags, went back and forth willy-nilly across the elegant rose-and-green patterned carpet.

Witherspoon started for the lift. But he'd not taken two steps when a soft voice called his name.

"Inspector Witherspoon."

Turning, he saw Lydia Modean standing next to a potted fern. Quite a large fern, he thought. He was sure she hadn't been standing there a moment ago.

"Good morning, Mrs. Modean," he said politely. "The constable and I were just on our way up to see you."

"I know," she replied. "The manager said you'd been by yesterday. I'm sorry we missed you." She cast a nervous glance towards the lift. "I knew you'd be back this morning. That's why I came down. I'd like to have a word with you before you speak to my husband."

"Of course, madam," he said.

She gestured toward the settee behind her. "If you'd be so kind, Inspector. We can sit here."

As they sat down, the inspector noticed that Mrs. Modean had positioned herself in such a way that she could see anyone coming down the central staircase or getting out of the lift. Barnes took a seat on the chair opposite and whipped out his notebook.

"Do you have to write it down?" she asked quietly.

Witherspoon was rather perplexed. They didn't *have* to write anything down. "The constable is taking notes, Mrs. Modean," he said gently, "not writing an official report."

She looked relieved. "Good. I mean, I don't even know if what I'm going to tell you has anything to do with this dreadful business."

"Why don't you just tell us, madam?" he said, giving her a reassuring smile. "And then we'll decide if it needs to be 'official.' "

Lydia drew a short, sharp breath and looked away. "I've known James Underhill for a long time," she said, turning back to the inspector. "Since I was eighteen. I hated him."

Witherspoon deliberately kept his expression blank. Though it was jolly difficult to think of this delicate creature hating anyone. "I see, madam. Would you tell me why?"

"This is hard, Inspector. Very hard." She swallowed. "To understand my feelings, you have to understand my circumstances."

"The same could be said for all of us," he said gently. "But please do go on."

"I came to London when I was eighteen. I had a job as a governess to a family in St. John's Wood. My own family was poor but well educated. That's why I was able to obtain the position. My father had been a schoolmaster before he became too ill to work, and I had to make my own way in the world. But I digress, sir. You're not interested in my personal misfortunes. As I said, I worked as a governess to a family named Peake. They were decent people, not unkind, but not unduly generous either. But I was very young, Inspector, and like many young women, I was silly and vain. My head was easily turned." She smiled sadly. "One day I was taking my charge for a walk in the park. A man approached me. He said I was the most beautiful woman he'd ever seen and asked if I would be willing to consider taking a position as an artists' model. Naturally, I told him no. I thought that was the end of the matter. But I was a fool. I should have told my employer about being accosted in the park the moment I got home. I shouldn't have even allowed this man to speak to me." She closed her eyes briefly.

"Gracious, madam, I don't see how you could have prevented it," Witherspoon said.

"I could have walked away," she said. "And I should have. The least I should have done was to go before he spoke to me in such intimate terms. Because my charge, Charlotte, told her mother what had happened. Oh, she was just a child of nine. She wasn't being malicious or deliberately trying to get me into trouble. But Mr. and Mrs. Peake were very angry. They told me in no uncertain terms that I was never, ever to carry on that kind of conversation with a strange man while in their employ. Especially when I had their daughter in my care. If I was approached again, I was to walk away."

"I take it you were accosted a second time?" Witherspoon asked, though he was fairly sure he could guess the answer.

"The following week. He came right up to me and started chatting like we were old friends." She laughed bitterly. "I told him to go away. But he didn't. To make matters worse, he followed me home."

"But surely your employers couldn't hold you responsible for this man's ungentlemanly behaviour," Witherspoon exclaimed.

"Oh, but they could and did." She shrugged. "I suppose I should have been flattered. When they sacked me they did tell me it wasn't my fault

I was pretty. But that's neither here nor there." She waved a hand dismissively. "The end result was that I found myself alone in London with very little money and very little prospects of getting another position as a governess."

"But surely they gave you a reference," Barnes blurted.

"They did," she replied. "But I'd gotten the job through the post, due to my father's influence. They'd never seen me before they hired me." She blushed self-consciously. "Mrs. Peake told me privately that if she'd seen me she'd never have given me the position."

"Please don't be embarrassed, Mrs. Modean," Witherspoon said gallantly. "You are a very beautiful woman. I suppose you were in a position where your appearance tended to be an obstacle to gainful employment." They both knew to what the inspector referred. Most wives would take one look at Lydia Modean and immediately find a dozen reasons not to hire her, regardless of how qualifed or well educated she was. Odd, the inspector thought, it was really the first time in his life he'd realized that being too attractive could cause one terrible difficulties.

"That's correct." She smiled, grateful for his understanding. "I couldn't go home. My father had died and my mother had been taken in by relatives. There wasn't room for me. So I tried to find work. But there was nothing, absolutely nothing. Of course, I ran out of money. I was just about to be turned out of my lodgings when the man who'd been the cause of all my troubles accosted me again. Only this time, when he asked if I was interested in a position, I told him yes. It was James Underhill. He got me jobs. Lots of them. I've posed for dozens of artists. That's how I met Tyrell."

"So your husband knows about your er . . . former occupation?"

She nodded. "Oh yes, he knows. He's bought a number of the paintings in which I was the model."

"Then I don't see why . . ." Witherspoon trailed off, not sure precisely what the right phrase should be.

"Why I wanted to meet you down here? Why I'm telling you all this? Why I don't want Tyrell to hear? It's very simple, Inspector. James Underhill was trying to blackmail me."

"But you've been living in America."

"He contacted me the day after we arrived here," she stated. "He demanded ten thousand pounds or he'd tell Tyrell about my past."

This time it was Barnes who asked, "But ma'am, you've just told us your husband knew. I'm assumin' that means he didn't much mind."

"He didn't mind," she insisted. "At least he didn't mind the legitimate artists. Not even the nudes."

"Nudes?" The word escaped the inspector's lips before he could stop it. "Oh, gracious, excuse me, Mrs. Modean. I meant no offense."

"None is taken," she replied.

"Then if your husband wasn't concerned about the uh . . . unclothed modeling jobs . . ." Witherspoon dithered ridiculously.

"He was going to tell Tyrell about the other one. The job I took when I was absolutely desperate." She closed her eyes and sobbed softly. "I posed for . . . for . . ."

The inspector was a policeman. He knew precisely what kind of pictures Mrs. Modean had posed for. "I think I know what you're trying to tell us, madam. Er, were the uh . . . pictures photographic plates or paintings?"

"It was only one and it was a plate. Underhill had it." She closed her eyes briefly. "It would hurt Tyrell unbearably if he found out. He's been so good to me. I love him so much. I'd do anything to spare him pain."

"Did you pay Underhill?" Barnes asked. He'd recovered faster than the inspector.

"No, I don't have that kind of money," she admitted. "But I was going to give him all the cash I had in exchange for the plate. But he was killed before I had the chance."

Chapter 7

Wiggins knew he was taking a terrible risk, but he didn't think he had much choice. He stopped at the edge of the strip of pavement on the side of the Grant home and peered down its gloomy length. If the layout of this house was like most Wiggins had seen in this part of London, then the kitchen, scullery, storerooms and the larders probably butted onto this side of the house. Halfway down the length of the walk, he could see an open door.

Wiggins took a hesitant step, grasped the package in his arms tighter and told himself not to be such a lily-livered coward — he was here to do a job and thanks to his own ingenuity, he had the means to get himself inside. If he was real lucky, he could do a bit of chatting with whoever happened to be about the place. If his luck run out, then the worst that could happen was he'd be given the boot. No, he reminded himself, getting booted off the premises wasn't the worst that could happen. Running into a copper that knew him or even, Wiggins gulped, running into the inspector himself made that pale in comparison. He'd just have to take care and look sharp.

Moving briskly, he started down the walkway. Coming to the doorway, he stuck his head in and saw that it opened into the scullery. A young woman, hardly more than a girl, was standing at a double sink just to the left of the doorway. She didn't notice Wiggins as she was up to her elbows in washing the mountain of pots, pans and crockery in the stone sink. He waited till she'd rinsed a bowl and sat it carefully on the wooden rack. He cleared his throat. "Excuse me, miss," he said.

Startled, the girl jumped back. "Who are you?"

"Sorry." He gave her his best smile. "I didn't mean to sneak up on ya. My name's Wiggins."

She cocked her head to one side and studied him. "If you're lookin' for work, it's not on. There's nothin' goin' here."

"I'm not lookin' for a position," he said. She was quite a pretty girl. Her hair, neatly plaited and tucked up under her maid's cap, was a lovely shade of brown, her eyes green and her skin, nicely flushed from the steam rising from the sink, a creamy shade of ivory. "I'm lookin' for someone."

"You'd best go round to the back door," she said, jerking her head toward the back garden. "The butler'll help you."

"I thought I was at the back door," Wiggins said. "I tried the one on the other side but it was locked tight."

164

"Not the side door." She shook her head. "That one's never used. There's a big door right round the back. It leads straight into the hall and the butler's pantry."

Shifting to one side, he deliberately brushed the brown paper wrapping of the parcel in his arms against the open door, drawing the girl's attention to it. "Can't you 'elp me?" he complained. "This is awfully 'eavy." He looked down at the package. "I'm lookin' for a . . ." He squinted, pretending he couldn't read the label.

"Well, who you looking for?" she demanded.

Helplessly, he glanced back up at her. "I can't read the blasted name. It's rubbed off the paper. What are the names of the girls that work 'ere?"

"My name's Cora," she began, "and there's a Rose and an Edith."

"That's it," he cried. "The one this is for! It's for you." As he'd doctored the name on the paper himself, he was quite sure that even if she could read, she'd not see through his ruse.

"What is it?" she asked suspiciously. But she took her arms out of the sink and reached for a tea towel. "And who'd be sending me somethin'?"

"I think it's from yer secret admirer," Wiggins said. "A feller paid me to bring it 'ere and gave me strict instructions not to give it to anyone but Cora."

Flattered, she broke into a huge smile. But she sobered instantly as she glanced at another closed door on the far side of the room. Through

165

there was the kitchen. "I don't know." She hesitated. "This is a right strict house. I'll get into trouble if I accept presents. You know how some people are about a girl havin' 'followers.' "

"But I think this is a nice tin of sweets," he persisted. "It'd be a shame to let 'em go to waste. Besides, the feller'll box me ears if I don't give it to ya."

She bit her lip in an agony of indecision. Then she brightened suddenly. "It's my afternoon out today. Can I meet ya somewhere? Then ya can give me the package?"

Wiggins pretended to consider the idea. But as he already knew from his chatting up the baker's delivery boy earlier today that it was some of the staff's day out today, he thanked his lucky stars he'd stumbled onto a girl who was going to be of some use to him. What he was doing wasn't very nice, pretending that this poor girl had a secret admirer and all, but it wasn't so awful either. And she would be getting a nice box of chocolates in the bargain. "Well, I don't rightly know. I'm busy, ya see . . . but still, ya look like a nice girl." He smiled brightly. "All right, then. Where do ya want me to meet you?"

"Do you know the Addison Station? It's just up the road a ways." Another worried glance at the kitchen. "I'll be there at half past two. Is that all right with you?"

Unable to believe his good luck, Wiggins nodded. "See ya then," he promised.

Wiggins spent the time before he was to meet

Cora talking to the shopkeepers in the neighborhood. Chatting them up wasn't risky at all. Everyone in the neighborhood was talking about the murder and everyone had an opinion about it too.

"Well, we weren't at all surprised there was murder done there," the stout shopkeeper said, jerking her head in the direction of the Grant house. "Mind you, my first thought was that it was probably some poor, honest merchant trying to collect his money. But of course, it wasn't, was it? It was some artist fellow or some such nonsense." She snorted in disgust. "Just like the Grants, isn't it? Always puttin' on airs and actin' like gentry. Well, I say gentry pays their bills. But they've not paid us what they owe, have they, Bert?" she yelled to a skinny man who was busy refilling the potato bins. "All toffee-nosed she is too, that Mrs. Grant. Not at all like her sister, Miss Collier. She's a nice one, she is. But that Mrs. Grant, she's no better than she ought to be, is she, Bert?" Bert didn't appear to feel it necessary to answer his wife's questions. He picked up a basket of cabbages and began plopping them into the bin next to the spuds.

"Do you know she actually had the nerve to come in here and have a go at me because I refused to send any more vegetables to the house?" the shopkeeper continued. "The nerve of the woman."

"Really?" Wiggins pretended to be shocked.

"Well, I told her she had to pay her bill, didn't

I, Bert? But did she? Oh no, too good to pay the likes of us, isn't she?"

"Maybe she didn't have the money," Wiggins suggested, more to keep the greengrocer talking than for anything else.

She scoffed. "Don't be daft, boy. The likes of her always has money. She's got enough to be out flouncing about in hansom cabs and toing and froing with all them fancy pictures she and her husband collect. Well, I say let 'em sell a few of them off and pay her bills. That's what I say, don't I, Bert?"

Wiggins's ears pricked. "When did you see Mrs. Grant out in a hansom?"

The woman pursed her lips, her round face creased in concentration. "It was the day that poor bloke got poisoned." She leaned closer and poked him in the chest with one short, sausage-shaped finger. "That very morning, in fact. Isn't that so, Bert?"

"What do you think, sir?" Barnes asked the inspector as they climbed the carpeted stairs to the second floor of the hotel. Mrs. Modean, after bringing herself under control, had gone upstairs a few moments earlier. It had been tacitly understood that none of them would allude to the earlier meeting.

Witherspoon winced visibly. "I don't quite know what to think," he admitted. "She certainly had a motive for wanting Underhill dead."

"But she claims she was going to pay him off,"

168

Barnes commented. "If she was going to pay him, why would she kill him? It's not like he could blackmail her indefinitely. She and her husband are going back to San Francisco soon and Underhill knew that."

"We only have her word that she was going to pay." Witherspoon gulped air into his lungs as they reached the top of the stairs. "And, of course, it's one thing to say it — it's quite another to actually have the money to do it."

"But she's rich."

"Her husband's rich," the inspector corrected. "For all we know, she has to account for every penny she spends."

They walked briskly down the hall, their footsteps making little noise against the thick maroon carpet.

"There it is." Barnes pointed to the door of room number twenty-two, then walked over and rapped lightly on the glossy wood.

From inside, they heard the soft murmur of voices. A second later Tyrell Modean, his lean, handsome face somber but not unfriendly, opened the door wide. "Good day, gentlemen," he said in his soft American drawl. "Come in. We've been expecting you." He moved back and ushered them into an elegant sitting room.

Lydia Modean, as composed as the Queen herself, sat on a cream-and-maroon striped settee next to the fireplace on the other side of the large room. "Hello, Inspector, Constable," she said politely.

"Good day, madam," Witherspoon replied, impressed by her composure. Barnes nodded.

"Please sit down," she said, pointing to a matching love seat and pair of chairs opposite the settee. "There's no reason we can't be civilized about this."

"We're only going to be asking you a few questions," the inspector said. "I don't think we'll be taking up too much of your time."

"That's very good of you, sir." Modean sat down on the settee next to his wife. He took her hand. "But we're prepared to give you as much time as you need. I apologize for not being here yesterday, but we had some rather important things to do. But you're not interested in my personal business, Inspector, and I'll get right to the point. I'll admit straight out that I didn't have much liking for James Underhill, but he didn't deserve to die like that."

"No one deserves to be murdered, sir," Witherspoon agreed. "Now, I know you've given us a statement already, but I've a few more details I'd like clarified. Was Mr. Underhill present when you arrived at the Grant house?"

Tyrell thought about it for a moment. He looked at his wife. "I don't remember seeing him, do you?" She shook her head negatively. "I think our answer has to be no, Inspector," he said, "unless he was there and in another room."

Witherspoon expected that reply. But he'd wanted to ask anyway. Sometimes asking obvious questions got surprising answers. "Do you recall what time Mr. Underhill did arrive?"

"Not really." Tyrell let go of his wife's hand and crossed his arms over his chest. "I was probably in the study with Neville Grant and I think Lydia had already gone outside with Mrs. Grant."

"How long were you in Mr. Grant's study?" Barnes asked.

"No more than ten minutes, when we went out to the garden. James Underhill was there with Arthur Grant. But I had the impression they'd only just arrived."

Barnes, who'd brought out his notebook, flipped back a few pages. "When you were in Mr. Grant's study, did you hear anyone coming in the front door?"

Modean looked surprised by the question. "Not that I recall," he began. "Why?"

"Because, sir" — Barnes frowned at his own handwriting — "according to the servants, no one remembers letting James Underhill in that afternoon."

"You mean he didn't come in with Arthur Grant?" Lydia asked.

"Arthur Grant was home that afternoon," Witherspoon replied. "He'd been up in his room since lunch, sleeping. He remembers hearing the door knocker twice. Once, earlier in the afternoon, when a police constable arrived asking for the whereabouts of a young woman, and again when the two of you arrived."

"I'm afraid I'm very confused," Lydia said.

"Are you saying a police constable was at the Grant house before Underhill was murdered?"

The inspector had no idea why he was telling them this bit of information. There was no evidence whatsoever that the alleged disappearance of Irene Simmons had anything to do with James Underhill's murder. But evidence or not, as his housekeeper had pointed out that morning at breakfast, a murder and a disappearance at the same house in the same week was stretching coincidence a bit too far. Besides, his conscience had been bothering him something terrible about that young woman. Since Underhill's murder, he'd completely pushed it to the back of his mind. Witherspoon wondered if he ought to speak so freely in front of what were possible suspects. At least in the Underhill matter. "Before I answer that," he said to them, "I need to ask you a question. Where were you a week ago yesterday? Around six o'clock in the evening."

Modean's jaw gaped. "Where were we?"

"That's right." He nodded encouragingly. "Were you here in London?"

"We were in Bristol," Lydia answered. "I don't have much family left, but there were a few people I wanted to see while I was here. You can check with the manager of the hotel. It was the Great Western Hotel. Inspector, could you please tell us what's going on?"

Witherspoon felt much better. If the Modeans were telling the truth, and he could find that out quickly enough, it meant they couldn't have had anything to do with Irene Simmons's disappearance. They weren't even in London when it was alleged to have taken place.

"I'm sorry to be so mysterious," he said. "But the reason I happened to be 'on the scene' so quickly the afternoon that Mr. Underhill was murdered is because I was on my way to the Grant house. You see, we've had a report that a young woman has gone missing. The last place where she was supposed to have gone was the Grants'."

Lydia and Tyrell looked at each other in disbelief. Finally, Tyrell asked, "Was this young woman a friend of the family?"

"No, actually, no one in the Grant house seems to have heard of her," he replied. "And all of them, including the servants, insist she was never there that evening."

"You think this woman's disappearance has something to do with the murder, don't you?" Lydia guessed. "That's why you asked us where we were last week."

"I'm afraid so," the inspector replied. "But the two events may not have anything to do with one another."

"That would be a pretty strange coincidence, don't you think?" Tyrell drawled.

"It would indeed," Witherspoon agreed quickly. "And though I know coincidences do happen, in this case, I feel the two events are connected."

"She was a model, wasn't she?" Lydia said.

Surprised, the inspector raised his eyebrows. "How did you know that, ma'am?"

She smiled knowingly. "It wasn't at all hard to figure out, Inspector. As a matter of fact, if I were a gambler, I'd wager that she went there after receiving a note promising her work. What's more, I know who sent her that note."

"Lydia," Tyrell warned. "Be careful of what you say. These men are policemen. I don't want them to get the wrong impression."

"Please, Mr. Modean," Witherspoon ordered. "Do let your wife finish." He looked at her. "Go on, please. A young woman's life may very well be at stake here." He turned to look at her. "Who sent her the note?"

Lydia smiled reassuringly at her husband and then turned her attention to the inspector. "James Underhill. It was one of his tricks. Believe me, I know. He did the same thing to me."

Wiggins spotted her as she hurried up the road toward the train station. He stepped away from the lamppost he'd been leaning on and dashed out to meet her. "I was afraid you'd changed yer mind," he said.

"Not likely." She shrugged. "I like my days out. Don't get 'em often enough if you ask me." As she spoke, her gaze was glued to the parcel in his hand. "Can I have it?"

From the eager expression on her face, Wiggins was afraid she'd snatch it and run off before he had a chance to talk to her. "Let's move over there," he said, jerking his head toward the railway station. "We're in the middle of the pavement 'ere."

"It's mine, isn't it?" Cora's eyes narrowed suspiciously.

"Course it is."

"Then just give it to me," she demanded. "I can take it with me."

"But won't they ask you questions if you come in with a nice package like this?" Wiggins's heart was sinking. The girl obviously wanted to be off.

"No. The household is strict, but they don't go snoopin' about in my parcels." She held her hand out.

" 'E said I was to watch ya open it," Wiggins fibbed. He didn't like lying to the girl. She was suspicious and he didn't much blame her. Lots of bad things could happen to a girl if she wasn't careful. "Come on, let's just step over there and ya can open it and I'll be able to tell 'im what 'e wants to 'ear and then everybody'll be happy as larks."

"All right." She turned and flounced over to stand next to the station building, taking care to keep to one side of the steps to stay out of the way. "Can I have it now?"

" 'Ere," he said, handing it to her. Frantically, he tried to think of something to keep her from leaving. He had to talk to her. He couldn't go back to this evening's meeting with nothing. And that little bit he'd gotten out of the shopkeeper wasn't worth repeating.

She stared at the parcel for a moment and then ripped off the paper. Her somber expression changed as the last of the wrapping came away and the delicate pink roses on the top of the tin came into view.

"Oh, my," she breathed, "these are lovely. I've never had anything like it."

Wiggins was delighted she liked them, so delighted that for a brief moment, he almost forgot their true purpose. "Good, I'm glad you're pleased . . ." He amended his sentence as she looked up at him, her expression sharp: "I mean, I can tell 'im you like 'em. He spent a pretty penny on 'em, that 'e did." Well, he thought, it was true, they had cost plenty. Not that he begrudged them. Thanks to their own mysterious benefactor at Upper Edmonton Gardens, he wasn't short of cash anymore.

"Who sent them?" she asked.

"Well," he said, "I don't rightly know."

"What do ya mean, you don't know?" she demanded.

"I didn't know the bloke, he just come up and give me a bob to bring 'em to ya." He stepped away from the building. "Now that I've done it, I've got to be off."

She took the bait. "Here, wait a minute. I've a few more questions for you. I thought you said he wanted you to watch me open it? Made a big fuss about it, you did. How's he goin' to know you watched me if you don't even know who he is?"

176

"I'm meetin' him at the pub this evening."

"Which pub?" she persisted. A mysterious suitor who had the money to buy a girl expensive chocolates was worthy of a few more minutes of her time.

"I've got to go," he insisted. He started purposefully down the road. "You can walk with me if you'd like," he called over his shoulder.

She hesitated for a fraction of a second. Then her curiosity got the better of her and she fell into step beside him. "What did this fellow look like?"

"He was about my height and my colorin'," Wiggins said cheerfully. " 'Andsome bloke, he was."

"It'll cost you a shilling, miss," the man said politely. "But it's well worth it."

Betsy gave him her best smile. She'd come all the way over to King Street, specifically to this art gallery, for one reason and one reason only. Information. She didn't mind spending a shilling to get it, either. But if the old woman had been right, she wouldn't have to. Her quarry was right in front of her. "I'm sure it is. Are you an artist?"

The man behind the counter blushed. He was quite young, but his light brown hair had already started to recede, his skin was pale and he had a goatee. "Well, yes, I am. I'm only working here so I can earn enough to buy my paint and canvas."

"Then your paintings aren't on exhibition?" She feigned disappointment.

177

He laughed. "Me? At Mr. J. P. Mendoza's St. James Gallery? Not yet. Maybe one day."

She smiled brightly. "Is Mr. Morante's work on view today?"

The boy-man gaped at her in surprise. "Morante?"

"Gaspar Morante," she replied. "Surely you've heard of him. He's a Spanish artist. Quite talented, I'm told."

"I've heard of him, all right," he shot back. "He's a friend of mine. I'm just surprised you've heard of him —"

"Why?" she interrupted, needing to keep control of the conversation. "Isn't he any good?"

"I didn't mean that," he said quickly, shaking his head in confusion, which was exactly the state Betsy wanted him in. "Alex is real good. He'll probably be famous one day, but he's not done much exhibiting."

"I was told his work was on display here" — she pointed to the door of the gallery — "and that the artist himself would be here as well. It's important that I speak to him. I've a commission for him."

"A commission? For Alex?" His eyes narrowed angrily. "Look, I don't know who you've been talkin' to, but he doesn't do that kind of thing anymore."

Betsy hid her surprise. "Well, I've been told he does," she countered, playing the situation by instinct. "If the price is right, that is."

"You've been talking to the wrong people,

then. Because it's not true."

"Why don't you let him decide that?" Betsy hoped she wasn't making a terrible fool of herself.

"I know what you want," the man sneered, "but you're not going to get it. Not this time. Now shove off before I call the police."

"Call the police? For what? Asking a few simple questions?"

"Don't act the innocent," he hissed. He leaned toward her menacingly, lifting the wooden partition that separated him from the customers.

"Hey, what're ya doin'?" Betsy jumped back a pace. She could make a run for it if she had to, but not before she got the most out of this fellow.

With the partition half raised, he hesitated and looked behind him toward the double front doors of the gallery. Obviously, leaving his post wasn't what he really wanted to do. "If you know what's good for you, you'll leave him alone," he warned. Slowly, he lowered the partition back into place. Betsy breathed a little easier.

"Like I said," he continued, his voice harsh with menace, "he doesn't do it. He never did. Those other times were accidents. He didn't know what was going on. He didn't do it deliberately. So go back and tell whoever it is you're working for that it's not on. Now get out of here."

Betsy suspected she'd gotten all she could get out of the man. He'd calmed down too much and seemed to have more control over his emotions.

She backed away. "All right, all right. Just tell him there's a job for him if he's interested."

"He's not. Now get off." He snarled.

"Why don't you let him speak for himself?" she challenged again. Maybe she could goad the man into telling her where he was.

He laughed harshly. "Do you think I'm a fool? Now get out of here and don't come back."

Betsy turned and walked away.

But she didn't go far. Only to the next corner where she ducked around a lamppost, whirled back toward the direction in which she'd just come and then planted herself there firmly. From where she stood, she could see the front of the gallery. She stood there for a moment, taking deep breaths and thinking about what had just happened.

Alex? Who was that? It had to be Gaspar Morante. Betsy rolled her hands into fists in an agony of indecision. She might be barking up the wrong tree. She'd no real proof that Morante had anything to do with Irene's disappearance. But she was tired of coincidences. Morante had disappeared from his lodgings on the same day Irene had. And now this. All she'd done was make a few casual remarks and Morante's friend had gone from being friendly to threatening. That was odd.

No, she thought, the fellow's behaviour was more than odd. He'd been scared. She'd seen it in his eyes even when she'd been backing up and getting ready to make a run for it herself. But why was he frightened? What did it mean?

She mentally debated what the wisest course of action would be. She could go back to Upper Edmonton Gardens and tell the others . . . yes, that's what she ought to do. Then she glanced up at the sky. The sun was moving steadily westward. It was getting late and the gallery closed at six. She couldn't make it all the way back home, explain what had happened and then get back here before her quarry got away. She couldn't risk it.

Betsy took a deep breath and made her decision. There was really only one sensible course of action. Surely Smythe and the others would understand.

A woman's life might be at stake.

"Can't say that there's many mournin' the feller," Blimpey said casually as he lifted his tankard and took a long sip. "Underhill weren't popular."

Smythe nodded, encouraging Blimpey to go on.

"Bit of a toff," Blimpey continued, "but as crooked a gent as has ever walked this earth. Came from a right good background," he said eagerly. "Like I said, a toff he was. This is where it gets interestin' — that's usually who he was swindling. His own kind."

"He was a swindler?" Smythe said.

"Not in the sense that ya normally think of it. He was kinda special in what 'e did." Blimpey wiped his mouth with the sleeve of his jacket. "Let me tell ya what I found out. Seems he was an artist's agent of some sort."

"I already knew that," Smythe said dryly. He forced himself to concentrate on his companion. But it was ruddy hard. His mind kept wandering back to Betsy. What was she up to now? She'd been blooming secretive about what she was doing today and he didn't like it.

"Yeah, well, what you don't know is that he wasn't exactly on the up-and-up. Most of his clients or customers or whatever didn't know it, either. But some of 'em did." Blimpey grinned and leaned forward eagerly. "And that's why his services were in such demand. The word is there's more than a few of 'em that asked the late Mr. Underhill to procure them a picture, and sometimes it's a picture just like one they already own . . . if you're gettin' my drift."

Smythe wasn't sure that he was. "You mean they want to buy a copy of their own painting from him?"

"No, no." He waved his hand impatiently. "Look, here's the way it works. Say you've got a nice painting and it's worth a lot of lolly. Then say you want to sell that painting but you don't really want to sell it 'cause you like it and it's worth so much cash. More importantly, it's likely to be worth even more if you can hang onto it for a few years. That's where Underhill came in. Seems he knew how to make sure you could sell your painting and keep it too."

"He forged paintings."

"*He* didn't," Blimpey replied. "He wasn't that good. He hired it done. Seems there's more than a few toffs that breathed a sigh of heartfelt relief when old Underhill got it. Now they don't 'ave to worry about him spillin' the beans over one toff sellin' one of his friends copies and not the real thing."

"Cor blimey, if what you're sayin' is true . . ."

"It is." Blimpey frowned, offended to the core. "I don't give bad information. Not for what you're goin' to be payin' me."

"Sorry." Smythe apologized for the slur on the man's professional dignity. "But there's somethin' I don't understand. If I was to sell ya a paintin' that's worth a lot of money and then give ya a forgery of that picture, what good would that do me? I couldn't sell the paintin' to someone else. People'd find out right quick if I was doin' things like that."

"That's what I thought," Blimpey said. "But art's not like other stuff . . . seems people don't ask a lot of questions sometimes. If I was to sell to you and then give you a fake, that means I could keep the real one. But let's say you was a foreigner, one of them Argentinians or Australians, and let's say I sold ya the fake and you quite happily took it back to WoggaWogga land or whatever and hung it up on yer wall to show off to all yer friends. None of them could tell the difference now, could they? And if I've got the real paintin' sittin' in a bank vault or an attic, I can put it in me will that the painting's to stay in the family. A generation or two passes and who's the wiser? The picture just keeps gettin' more and more valuable and the people with the fake think they've got the real thing too. By the time anyone sorts it out, odds are the toff what commissioned the forgery is dead and buried and not havin' to worry about it. And don't forget this — if you owned the forgery and you found out it was a fake, would you tell anyone?"

"I don't know," Smythe replied honestly. "What good would havin' a fake do ya?"

"Plenty." Blimpey grinned. "You could pass it on to someone else. People don't bother gettin' forgeries done of paintings that ain't worth a lot of money. And that ain't all," he continued. "Seems that Underhill didn't do it just for the lolly. Rumor has it that he was a bit of an odd duck about paintings and such." He snorted. "Seems to me the feller was downright daft. Some claim that he kept more than he'd sold and had it stashed away somewhere." He laughed. "Sounds to me like he was buildin' a nest egg. Probably goin' to make one last, grand bunco and then take off. Maybe the bloke wasn't so daft after all. Art usually goes up in value. A few paintings sold on the sly could keep a fellow in clover for a long time. Course, playin' about a bit with a paintin' or two ain't the worst of the man."

"There's more?" Smythe said incredulously.

"You can bet your front teeth there is," Blimpey said. He looked quickly over his shoulder to make sure they weren't being overheard and then, just to be doubly safe, he leaned across the small table. "Word 'as it that he'd hired some thugs to do a killin'."

Smythe went utterly still for a few moments. "Are ya sure?"

Blimpey, his expression somber, nodded. "Sure as you and I are sittin' 'ere havin' this nice little chat," he said. "I double-checked that bit, I can tell ya that. Underhill did it, all right. Word is he hired a couple of Mordecai's boys along about ten days ago. Paid a fair amount for it too. They was supposed to stab a woman and make it look like it was the work of that Ripper fellow." Blimpey grimaced. "Ugly, that was. Now, there was one I would'na minded seein' swing by his neck. Too bad the coppers was too ruddy stupid to catch 'im."

Smythe swallowed heavily. He had to ask. He had to know. "Did they do it? Did they murder her?"

Blimpey chuckled and leaned back. "Nah, they was goin' to, but somethin' went wrong. Far as I know the girl's still alive."

"What's her name?"

"Now that, I can't tell ya," Blimpey said. He held up his hand quickly as he saw Smythe open his mouth. "And I ain't trying to squeeze any more lolly out of ya," he protested. "I don't hold with murder, especially women. If I knew the girl's name I'd not only tell ya, I'd tell 'er too. I may have been a thief and a pickpocket once, but

185

that don't mean I got no morals. I know what's right. Separating a toff from 'is coin and sellin' a bit of information is one thing, but murder is somethin' else."

Smythe shut his mouth. Blimpey would tell him the girl's name if he knew it. Too bad he didn't. "Can you find out?"

Blimpey looked offended. "Is the Thames a river? Of course I can find out. I just couldn't find out before I had to meet ya 'ere now." His eyes narrowed to slits. "For yer information, I'm already workin' on it. It's not goin' to cost you a ruddy bob. As soon as I know who the lass is, you'll know too, and for that matter, so will the coppers."

Taken aback, Smythe stared at him with something akin to admiration. "Fair enough," he murmured. "Is there anythin' else?"

"Not yet." Blimpey downed the last of his drink. "I'll have more by tomorrow. Got to be on me way," he said, getting to his feet. "I'll send one of me lads with a message when I've more for ya." He nodded brusquely and turned toward the door.

"Blimpey." Smythe stopped him.

"What?"

"Be careful. Mordecai's boys are a pretty rough lot." They were worse than rough, Smythe thought. They were killers. Most of them did it for money, but some of them did it because they liked it.

Blimpey grinned. "I'm always careful, Smythe.

That's why I'm still alive and kickin'. Don't worry. I can handle Mordecai and his lot."

"They're killers, Blimpey," he warned.

"And for the most part, they're dumber than tree stumps." Blimpey laughed. "Don't worry, me friend. When the day comes that I can't outsmart a thug like Mordecai, I'll give up the game and retire to me country cottage."

Chapter 8

Betsy missed supper, but she did manage to make it back to Upper Edmonton Gardens before the meeting started.

Smythe, his face thunderous, was pacing the back hall. "Just where in the bloomin' blue blazes 'ave you been?" he demanded.

"I've got a good reason for being late," she told him tartly as she took off her hat and coat and dashed for the kitchen, "and I'll thank you not to glare at me like that."

"You missed supper," he hissed, outraged that not only was she late, but she didn't look in the least repentant for worrying him half to death.

"I'm the one who's going hungry tonight," she shot back, "so don't fret about it."

"Fret about it?" he snapped. "I'm not frettin', lass, I'm ruddy furious. I've been worried sick about ya."

The look in his eyes took the wind out of her sails. Suddenly contrite, she dropped her voice as they came in to the kitchen proper. "I didn't mean to be late," she explained, "and I'd not have you concerned for me, Smythe. But it couldn't be helped."

"Good evening, Betsy," Mrs. Jeffries called. She, like the others, was already seated around the table. "Mrs. Goodge has kindly kept a plate of food in the oven for you. Would you like to eat while we have our meeting?"

"No." Betsy smiled in relief. The thought of going without supper had been a bit depressing. She was hungry. "I can wait till afterward. I'm ever so sorry to keep everyone waiting, but it couldn't be helped. I think I might have a clue as to Irene's whereabouts."

"Excellent, Miss Betsy." Hatchet beamed. "I too learned something interesting which may help us to find the young lady. Which of us should go first, do you think?"

"Hold yer horses, now," Luty chimed in. "Who says you get to go first? I've found out plenty today too and it's about the murder."

"Well, I've got my bits and pieces to tell as well," Mrs. Goodge put in, "and if I do say so meself, they're pretty interestin'."

"So do I," Wiggins added.

From the eager expressions on everyone's faces, Mrs. Jeffries suspected they all had something to report. "Why don't we take it in turns," she suggested. "As we've all agreed that there is a strong possibility the murder and Irene's disappearance are linked, I suggest we hear what Betsy and Hatchet have to say first." She smiled at Betsy. "Why don't you start? We're all rather curious as to why you were so late."

"All right. You know how yesterday I found out that that artist who first hired Irene, Gaspar Morante, had up and disappeared?" she began. "Well, what I forgot to mention was that I had a clue as to how I might find out where he'd got to."

Smythe snorted. "Forgot to mention it, did ya?"

Betsy ignored him. "Anyway, today I found out a bit more. Not just about him disappearin', but about the way he'd disappeared as well. He left his studio about five o'clock on that day, took off in a ratty old Bachelors Brougham and hasn't been seen since."

"Was it his carriage?" Smythe asked, getting interested in her information in spite of being so niggled at the girl that he couldn't think straight.

"He doesn't own it." Betsy shook her head. "That's why the neighbors noticed it when he drove off. Wasn't much of a driver, either."

"What's so odd about him goin' off in a brougham?" Mrs. Goodge asked. "Lots of people do that, even ones that aren't all that rich. Carriages can be hired, you know."

"But Morante's as poor as a church mouse," Betsy objected. "He barely makes ends meet. Then all of a sudden he up and takes off in a carriage of all things, even a ratty old one like the one he was driving that night. What's more, he left with people owing *him* money. Two days after he went, a gallery owner showed up at his studio wanting to pay Morante for selling one of his paintings."

"Did anyone have any idea where Morante

190

went?" Hatchet asked.

"No, but that brings me to where I was today," Betsy said. "The old woman I talked to gave me the name of one of his friends, another artist. But when I went to see him today, he got all het up and started acting right strange. He kept going on about someone called Alex and saying that 'Alex doesn't do that anymore.' So I decided the fellow was acting so odd and rattled that maybe I ought to keep an eye on him."

"Keep an eye on 'im 'ow?" Smythe asked.

"I waited till he left work," Betsy clarified eagerly, "and then I followed him. That's why I was so late this evening. He didn't get off till six. I know something odd's going on too, because he kept looking over his shoulder and acting like he was expecting to be followed."

"You *were* following him," Mrs. Jeffries pointed out.

"But he didn't know that." Frustrated, Betsy frowned. "I made out that he'd scared me off."

"Scared ya off?" Smythe yelped. "What'd 'e do to ya?"

"Nothing, just got a bit shirty when I started asking about Morante." Betsy waved at him impatiently. "It wasn't me he was afraid might be following him, I know that. He never saw me, I made sure. But he was still walking like a man keeping one eye out for the grim reaper."

"What makes you think this man will help you find Irene?" Luty asked. "Seems to me there could be half a dozen reasons why this Morante skedaddled out of town."

"His name isn't Gaspar Morante," Hatchet said smoothly, his full attention focused on Betsy. "Well, it is, but that's only part of it. His real name is Alessandro Gaspar Morante de Montoya. That's probably why the man you spoke with referred to him as Alex."

"How did you find that out?" Betsy was impressed.

Hatchet grinned. "The same way you do, Miss Betsy, with my wits and my brain."

Luty snorted.

"I also found out that Morante seems to have come into some money recently," Hatchet continued seriously.

"From sellin' his paintings?" Wiggins guessed.

"Well, one could say that." Hatchet hesitated. "The rumor I heard was that Morante copied old masters, which were then sold as the genuine article." He sat back and folded his arms over his chest. "The man he worked for was James Underhill."

There was a long moment of silence as everyone digested that piece of information.

"And now that Underhill's dead," Smythe mused, "Morante's back to bein' as poor as a church mouse. That lets him out as a suspect. A man doesn't kill the goose that's layin' the golden egg."

"In most cases, your reasoning would be quite accurate," Hatchet said. "But we can't eliminate Morante as a suspect . . ."

"I didn't even know he was on the list," Mrs. Goodge grumbled.

". . . because according to my sources," Hatchet continued, "Morante had no idea he was doing forgeries."

"No idea? But how is that possible?" Mrs. Jeffries asked. This case was certainly getting complex. If it took any more twists or turns, she might be reduced to writing out a cast of characters and a full complement of motives just to keep everything straight in her own mind.

"Underhill had duped Morante into doing the forgeries," Hatchet explained. He leaned his elbows on the table and steepled his hands together. "Supposedly, he went to Morante and told him he had a client who wanted copies of several paintings done. The client was going to put the originals in a bank vault for safekeeping and hang the copies up in his home. It sounds a reasonable enough sort of plan. Especially as Underhill was a broker known to have wealthy clients."

"But why would Morante agree?" Wiggins asked. "Didn't 'e 'ave 'is own paintin' to worry about?"

"Morante was desperate for money," Hatchet clarified. "His own work wasn't selling very well, so he agreed to do the copying."

"And he didn't know what he was doin' was forgery?" Luty said incredulously.

"I suppose he ought to have known" — a smile flitted around Hatchet's mouth — "but as it's quite common for artists to train in their craft by copying the old masters, somehow I imagine that they don't quite see it in that light. Be that as it may, Morante did the paintings and took the money. But when Underhill came to him again, about two weeks ago, with another client who wanted to do the same thing, he got suspicious."

"About what?" Mrs. Goodge yelped. "Sounds like good sense to put a valuable painting in the bank vault and hang a copy on the wall."

"It is," Hatchet said softly. "But Morante was suspicious that Underhill's clients weren't the rightful owners of the paintings at all. In short, he accused Underhill of having him paint forgeries and either selling them outright to unsuspecting buyers or using the forgeries while he stole the originals."

Smythe's breath hissed sharply through his teeth. Now it was starting to make a bit of sense. "How long ago was it that Irene Simmons last posed for Morante?"

Puzzled, Betsy shrugged. "I don't know. Why?"

"It was just over two weeks ago," Mrs. Jeffries said. "I found that out today when I went back to Nanette's for another chat. As a matter of fact, her posing for Morante was the last job she had before she received the mysterious note summoning her to the Grant house on the night she disappeared."

"Maybe she overheard somethin' she should'na?" Wiggins suggested somberly. "Maybe she overheard Morante and Underhill

194

havin' a go at each other over forgin' them paint-ings?"

Mrs. Jeffries eyed the footman speculatively. She'd been thinking along those very lines her-self. "I think you might be on to something," she mused, half thinking aloud as she spoke. "If Morante knew that Irene had overheard his conversaton with Underhill, that would give him not only a motive to kidnap her, but also a reason for getting rid of Underhill. Irene Simmons could go to the police. I don't know what the penalty for art forging is, but I expect it's most unpleasant. But more importantly, if it was ever learned that he'd copied paintings, his own work would be impossible to sell. No reputable gallery or agent would have anything to do with him."

"But how could he have gotten the poison into that tin of mints?" Mrs. Goodge asked. "I know we've already agreed that the killer didn't have to be at the Grant house the day that Underhill ate the mints, but he'd have to be able to get close enough to Underhill to tamper with his mints somehow. I don't see how Morante could have done that, not if he was openly squabbling with Underhill."

"But maybe he wasn't openly at odds with him," Mrs. Jeffries continued, her voice re-flecting her growing enthusiasm for this solu-tion. "Perhaps he pretended that all was well between them; perhaps he even apologized for their 'argument.' Then, all he had to do was buy a tin of mints, doctor a few of them with a solution of cyanide and then slip them into Underhill's coat pocket whenever he pleased."

"But when could he have done it?" Betsy asked. "Morante disappeared the same day Irene did and that was a week before the murder."

"He could have done it at any time," the housekeeper replied, absently brushing an errant bread crumb off the tabletop. "Underhill carried his mints in his coat pocket. All Morante would have had to do was find an opportunity to make the switch. It could have happened anywhere — a restaurant, an art gallery, anywhere. No one would be any the wiser. Then, all Morante had to do was wait until Underhill ate the poisoned mints. That would explain the time gap between his kidnapping of Irene and the death of Underhill."

Luty angled her head to one side and sighed dramatically. "I hate to be drapin' crepe on yer idea, Hepzibah, but like you've said yerself, hadn't we better git us some facts before we go makin' wild guesses that might have us runnin' around chasin' our tails and not the killer?"

Taken aback, Mrs. Jeffries simply stared at her. "You think my theory is flawed?"

"It's jest fine, for a theory," Luty replied. "But hadn't we better stick to facts? First of all, we don't know for sure Irene heard anything when she was at Morante's, and even if she did, seems to me a lot of time passed between the eavesdroppin' and the disappearance."

"But I've explained the time gap," Mrs. Jeffries

protested, though Luty made a valid point. Perhaps she oughtn't be so eager to accept a theory just because it made sense on the surface.

"You've explained why there was a week between the kidnapping and the murder," Luty agreed, "but that don't explain why Morante waited to git his hands on Irene. If I recall rightly, you all said Irene was supposed to have overheard this conversation two weeks ago. That would mean that Morante, knowing that model had heard everythin' and had the power to ruin him, let her flit about London free as a bird while he did nothing. Then almost a week after her hearin' this damagin' information, he decides to kidnap her. Seems to me that's a bit like closin' the barn door after the horses have run off."

Mrs. Jeffries's shoulders slumped. Luty was right. The theory, lovely as it was, simply had too many holes in it. "I see your point. I'm basing my theory on unproven assumptions. Furthermore, my theory doesn't explain why Morante would kidnap Irene. Why not just murder her as well?"

"That don't mean you ain't right," Luty said quickly. "Jest because it's dumb don't mean people don't do it. Could be this here Morante feller's as thick as two short planks and it took him a week to do his plottin' and his plannin' to git his hands on the girl. I'm jest sayin' we've got to be careful, that's all. As to why he'd kidnap Irene and not kill her . . ." She shrugged. "Well, lots of men are kinda squeamish about doin' somethin' like that to a woman."

"You're being very kind, Luty," Mrs. Jeffries said. "But you've no need to try and spare my feelings. My idea is really quite silly. Morante may know something about the murder and Irene's disappearance. I believe it's in our interest to try and find him, but other than that, well, we'll just have to wait and see what he knows."

"This information does provide the necessary link between the murder and the disappearance," Hatchet said. "I think we can safely assume the two events are definitely connected. But I agree with you, Mrs. Jeffries. I think we'd better wait until we locate Morante before we make anymore theoretical assumptions."

"I'm not so sure about that," Smythe said flatly. He was as confused as everyone else. But he wasn't going to worry about it yet. They'd sort it out in the end. They always did. "Seems to me Mrs. Jeffries might be on the right track after all."

"And how do you know that?" Mrs. Goodge asked. She was a bit put out because the bits and pieces she'd picked up today were beginning to pale into insignificance compared to the others.

"Because I found out from my sources that James Underhill is a killer himself," he replied, his tone disgusted. " 'E 'ired a couple of thugs to murder a woman. Paid plenty for it too, only somethin' went wrong and the woman's not dead. That's why I'm thinkin' there might be somethin' to Mrs. Jeffries's theory. Seems to me that this Morante feller could've found out the same."

"Do you know who this woman was?" Mrs. Jeffries asked.

"Not yet," the coachman replied, "but I'm workin' on it."

"It's probably Irene Simmons," Wiggins guessed.

"That's what I'm thinkin'," Smythe agreed, "but I won't know for sure until tomorro—" He broke off as footsteps sounded on the back stairs. Everyone turned toward the hall just as the inspector, with Fred at his heels, bounded into the kitchen. "Gracious," he said, coming to a halt at the doorway. "I didn't know we had company."

Mrs. Jeffries rose quickly. "Luty and Hatchet only stopped in a few moments ago, sir."

Witherspoon's face mirrored his delight. He quite liked the eccentric American and her butler. "I say," he said cheerfully as he hurried toward the table, "do you mind if I join you? I could do with some company this evening. This horrid case I'm working on just won't let me relax."

Inspector Witherspoon was in fine form the next morning as he stepped out of the hansom in front of James Underhill's lodging house. He'd slept like a baby, eaten a huge breakfast and was brimming with new ideas about this case. Odd, how just an hour or two spent in convivial conversation with one's household could send the mind moving in so many interesting directions. Why, he thought, as he marched up the walkway to the front door, he'd not have considered

199

coming back here if it hadn't been for an odd comment made by Wiggins.

Witherspoon knocked on the front door. Of course, Smythe's information was also important, the inspector told himself while he waited for someone to answer the door. Between his coachman and his footman, he'd come up with quite a number of things to do this morning.

The door opened and a middle-aged woman, her face set in grim lines, peeked out. "Yes?"

He doffed his bowler hat. "Good morning, madam. I'm Inspector Witherspoon. Are you the landlady of this establishment?"

"I am." She opened the door wider. "The police have already been here," she accused. "They said they were finished and I could rent his rooms out."

"Oh dear," Witherspoon replied. "You haven't cleaned them out yet, I hope?" There was no need to clarify what they were talking about. Both of them knew it was Underhill.

"I've been up there," she said, jerking her chin toward the staircase behind her, "but that lazy Feniman hasn't come round yet and I can't move that stuff without him. He claimed he'd be here at eight, and just look, it's gone past nine and the shiftless fool still isn't here."

Silently thanking the hapless Feniman for his tardiness, the inspector stepped past the landlady into the foyer. "If you don't mind, I'd like to have a quick look around before you remove his things."

"Help yerself." She shrugged. "Though I don't know why you coppers can't get it right the first time."

Witherspoon started up the stairs. "I'll try not to inconvenience you, madam."

"You've already inconvenienced me," she snapped. "Feniman was here the second time your lot come around to search and he had his wagon with him. If that peeler hadn't wasted the whole afternoon, I'da had them rooms cleaned and rented by now."

He stopped and turned to look at her. "Second time, madam?" he queried. "But the police have only been here once."

She shook her head in denial. "There was one here the other day, claimed he was with Scotland Yard."

"What did he look like?"

She shrugged. "Scrawny feller. Pale skinned, he was. Had wispy blond hair. He was here searchin' them rooms for a good two hours. Jumpy, he was. He about went through the ceiling when I come in to ask him if he was finished."

Witherspoon's heartbeat accelerated. He quickly cast his mind to the faces of those involved with this case. After a moment, he suspected he knew who had been in the victim's rooms. "Thank you, madam," he said. "You've been most helpful. However, in the future, if someone else claims they are the police, would you please be so kind as to send for me before you allow them into the late Mr. Underhill's rooms?"

"How many more coppers do you expect'll be around?" she yelped. "I'm wantin' to rent them rooms out."

"I don't think anyone else will come," he said hastily. "But in the event someone does, please contact me immediately."

She shrugged and wandered off down the hallway, still muttering about the lazy Feniman and the bloody coppers. The inspector continued up the stairs. The door leading to Underhill's quarters was open. He stepped inside and slowly let his gaze survey the sitting room.

The room was quite beautiful. Not just nicely appointed or adequately decorated, but stunningly lovely.

Brilliant jewel colors of a large Persian carpet covered polished hardwood floors. The settee and love seat grouped invitingly around a small rosewood table were upholstered in a deep, rich rose fabric that went beautifully with the color of the flowers in the cream-and-pink chintz curtains. In the far corner a Queen Anne armchair stood next to a dainty seventeenth-century single drawer desk, the top of which was bare. But it wasn't the elegance of the quarters that made one stop and take pause. It was the paintings. Dozens of them — they covered the walls so thickly one couldn't really make out what color the wallpaper might be. There were large ones in glittering gilt frames, small watercolors surrounded by simple wood and some that had no frames at all.

Shaking his head in wonder, the inspector advanced into the room. There was no one particular style or period to the collection. Bright, colorful landscapes hung next to somber portraits from the eighteenth century. Pastoral scenes, sailing ships, raging seas, Italian madonnas and even one or two nudes that made the inspector blush hung in uneven rows along all four walls. The room had been aesthetically designed to appeal to both the eye and the mind.

Witherspoon shook his head sadly. James Underhill, for all his faults as a human being, had been a man who'd understood the compelling lure of visual beauty.

"Excuse me, sir."

Witherspoon started and whirled around. "Oh, hello, Constable," he said to Barnes. "I see you got my message."

Barnes, his mouth gaping in wonder and his expression awed, stepped further into the room. "Yes sir," he muttered. "I got here as quickly as I could. Have you ever seen the like, sir?"

"Not outside a museum," Witherspoon replied honestly. "It's quite a spectacle, isn't it?"

"Are they all real, sir?" Barnes asked. "I mean, are they valuable . . . or copies or what?"

"I'm not sure," Witherspoon replied. "But from what we know of our investigation into Mr. Underhill's finances, I can't quite see them being valuable. According to both his solicitor and his bank manager, he'd not much money."

"Maybe this is why," Barnes said, grinning and jerking his head toward the far wall. "Could be the man loved art more than anything." He sobered quickly. "What are we doin' here, sir? The lads have already searched the place. They found nothing of interest, sir. No notes, no threatening letters, nothing which gives —"

"Precisely," Witherspoon interrupted with relish. "That's the whole problem. There should have been. Underhill conducted his business from here — he didn't have a proper office and he was a broker or an agent of some sort. At least enough of one to make a living at it and be able to afford all this." He swept his arm in an arc that included the paintings.

"I see what you're gettin' at, sir." Barnes nodded in understanding. "There should have been ledgers and bills of sales or invoices. But there aren't." He slowly turned and surveyed the room, and then he walked quickly to the desk in the corner. He opened the drawer, reached inside and pulled out a slender sheaf of pristine white notepaper. "Nothing here but his stationary. How did the man conduct his business?"

"That's what we have to find out," Witherspoon said cheerfully, remembering what Wiggins had inadvertently said the night before. "There's also another matter we need to investigate." His manner darkened perceptibly as he remembered the rather frightening message that Smythe had given him. Really, he wasn't sure he liked his staff being the recepients of such terrifying information. Even if they were just passing it along to him. He'd never forgive himself if one of his household were ever hurt or endangered by Witherspoon's profession. But right now wasn't the time to concern himself with that matter. It would be investigated thoroughly as soon as he and the constable finished here. Then again, he thought, maybe there was nothing to it. Perhaps his coachman had merely been accosted by one of those odd people who seem to come out from everywhere whenever they read about a murder.

"What other matter, sir?" Barnes asked.

"Huh? Oh." He smiled apologetically at the constable. "Nothing, Barnes. I mean, I'll tell you all about it on our way to the Grant house."

"We're going back there, sir?"

"Yes, we've got to have a word with Arthur Grant. But before we do that, I suggest we look for a key."

"To what, sir?" Barnes asked.

"To Underhill's office," the inspector replied.

"But he didn't have one, sir."

"That's just it, Constable. He has to have kept his paperwork somewhere. There has to be a room or a cupboard or a file cabinet or something."

"Maybe he kept it in his head," Barnes suggested.

"I doubt that, Barnes," Witherspoon replied, his attention caught by a lovely painting of a windswept beach. "His clients would no doubt have demanded receipts and invoices."

Barnes wasn't so sure. But nevertheless, he and the inspector set about looking for a key.

Mrs. Jeffries absently picked up her teacup and took a sip. Behind her, Mrs. Goodge closed the oven door with a bang. The housekeeper smiled to herself. The cook was still sulking because of the inspector's interruption last night. She'd been the only one of them who hadn't been able to get her information out in the open with their dear employer sitting there.

Mrs. Jeffries was actually quite proud of the staff. They'd done splendidly. Betsy, her eyes innocently wide, had asked the inspector how the hunt for Irene Simmons was proceeding. Witherspoon, after blustering a moment, had finally admitted that it wasn't going well at all. The murder of James Underhill was taking all of his time.

"Oh well, sir," Betsy had said, "I suppose then the bit of gossip I've picked up won't do you any good."

"Gossip?" Witherspoon had popped up in his chair like a marionette having his string pulled. He was well aware of the importance of gossip. "About Irene Simmons? By all means, Betsy, do tell me what you've heard."

The maid had outdone herself, making up a convuluted tale of back-fence whispers, shop assistants who'd heard this and that and delivery boys who'd stopped her on the high street because she worked for the inspector. Betsy had managed to get the whole tale of Morante's disappearance and connection to Irene straight into the inspector's listening ears.

"You see, sir," she'd concluded brightly, "everyone knows you're the most brilliant detective in all of Scotland Yard. That's why they're always stopping me and telling me things. You know how it is, sir. They want to be important but none of them wants to come to you themselves. They're afraid of looking foolish."

Mrs. Goodge slapped a round of bread dough onto the flour-covered marble slab on the far end of the table. Making a fist, she punched it hard enough to rattle the teapot.

Mrs. Jeffries winced. "Now, now, Mrs. Goodge, we're going to have another meeting this evening. You'll be able to tell us your bits and pieces then. You mustn't upset yourself."

"Who says I'm upset?" She rolled half the dough on top of itself and kneaded it with the palm of her hand. "It just seems to me the inspector didn't have to go runnin' up to bed before I had a chance to say my piece."

"But it was after ten o'clock. He was getting very tired."

"Humph." She snorted, taking another whack at the dough. "He had plenty of time to listen to Wiggins goin' on about Arthur Grant and Smythe's tale of Underhill's murder plot."

"Only because Wiggins's information dovetailed so very nicely with Smythe's," the housekeeper replied calmly. Really, it had been quite remarkable how the coachman had managed to get his information said. He'd been quite bold about it, claiming that he'd been stopped on his way out of the stables and told by a man that James Underhill had plotted a woman's murder. Witherspoon had been amazed. Of course he'd asked Smythe what this informant looked like. Smythe, always a fast thinker, said he couldn't say. The informant had kept to the shadows of the stable. The only other thing the alleged informant said was that he'd followed Smythe deliberately because he knew he worked for the inspector.

"My information would have dovetailed nicely too." Mrs. Goodge picked the entire round of dough up, turned it over and slapped it back on the marble. "If I'd had a chance to tell it. And Wiggins's bits didn't have anything to do with what Smythe told us," she continued, taking another swing at the hapless mound in front of her. "He just pretended like it did. All he said was that some silly maid at the Grant house had told him that Arthur Grant was all het up about something on the day that Underhill was killed." She snorted again. "If I'd had a chance, I could have told him what's what. I know what Grant was up to. That's what my sources told me."

Mrs. Jeffries put the cup she'd just picked up back down. She knew she should wait for the others, but this might be important. "What?"

"You want me to tell you now?" the cook

asked. "Without the others?"

The housekeeper hesitated, but finally couldn't resist the temptation. "Yes. The day is still young. Tell me what you know. It may influence where I go and who I talk with today."

Mrs. Goodge smiled slowly. "All right, then. If you think it's important."

"I do," Mrs. Jeffries assured her. "I think it's very important."

"Well, there's two things, actually." Mrs. Goodge plopped the battered dough into a bowl. Wiping her hands on her apron, she sat down next to the housekeeper. "The first was that Mary Grant's family once had one of the best art collections in the country, but it was sold off piece by piece to keep a roof over their heads."

"When was this?" Mrs. Jeffries didn't remind the cook that she'd already shared this information. She didn't wish to hurt her feelings or interrupt her.

"Years ago, well before she married Mr. Grant. By the time he come along, all that was left was the paintings she used as a dowry."

"Strange that she'd use such valuable paintings to marry a man like Neville Grant," the housekeeper mused. "From what the inspector said, Mrs. Grant isn't hideously ugly."

"No, she's not hideous," the cook said, "but she's sharp tongued and a bit of a shrew. There weren't many that would have her, dowry or not. And she was tired of bein' a spinster. You'd think that would make her more understanding about her sister, wouldn't you? I mean, she wanted to marry so why shouldn't Helen want to marry too?"

"Perhaps she didn't wish her sister to get her hopes up," Mrs. Jeffries suggested. "The inspector did say that Mary Grant was convinced that Helen's engagement was all a figment of Helen's imagination."

"I don't think that's true," Mrs. Goodge said. "Not after what Wiggins told us."

Puzzled, the housekeeper looked at her. She couldn't recall Wiggins making any comment about Helen Collier. "I'm afraid I don't know what you mean."

"Don't you remember what the lad said Cora had told him?" Mrs. Goodge said. "Cora said that a couple of days before the murder, Miss Collier bumped into Underhill at her bank. Well, that proves it, doesn't it?"

"Oh, that." Mrs. Jeffries nodded. "Yes, I remember now. But I'm afraid I still don't understand. What does that have to do with Helen's alleged engagement?"

"Everything," Mrs. Goodge exclaimed. "My sources told me that Helen Collier goes to her bank once a month to withdraw the money she'll need. She also goes to have a look-see at her paintings. She owns three Caldararos as well. Underhill met her there but I'd bet my next quarter's wages it wasn't an accident. I think he met her there so he could see those paintings for himself. Having seen them, I think he made up his mind to marry her so he could get his hands on 'em."

Mrs. Jeffries stared at her for a long moment. "My goodness, you might be right. Of course, knowing what we know of the dead man, he'd want to make sure the paintings were real before he committed himself to marriage. If, of course, he was genuinely considering marriage to the woman."

"No reason for him not to," Mrs. Goodge said bluntly. "Underhill wasn't any spring chicken himself. Man gets to be his age, probably starts wondering who's going to be taking care of him and doin' his fetchin' and carryin' for him when he gets old. Remember, he was gentry too. But gentry with no money. It's not like he'd have been welcomed by many women of his own class. Not as poor as he was. Helen Collier did have a small income and three very valuable paintings to her credit. More importantly, she was willing."

"Yes, quite." Mrs. Jeffries was quite impressed with the cook's analysis. "And the second thing you learned?"

"Oh, that." She waved her hand impatiently. "I heard some gossip that Arthur Grant needed something from Underhill. Needed it desperately. That's why he invited him around to tea that day. He was waiting for Underhill to broker some kind of deal for him."

Chapter 9

This time, Betsy was prepared. She dodged behind a cooper's wagon as her quarry crossed the wide pavement of the railway station. He walked right on past the entrance to the cloakroom, stopped in front of the door to the station proper, glanced once over his shoulder and then ducked inside.

She gave him a few moments to get ahead and then dashed in after him. He was heading for the platforms. Betsy started to follow, realized she didn't have a ticket and then glanced anxiously around looking for the notice board. It was over the ticket kiosk. Lifting her skirts, she rushed toward it, praying a train wasn't just now pulling out with her prey already on it.

There were three trains leaving in the next half hour, two locals and an express. She dithered for a moment, wondering which he'd be on and then made up her mind. She bought a ticket for the one leaving right away and raced for the platform at a run, telling herself that the worst that could happen is she'd have to go through this again tomorrow if she was wrong. But to her way of thinking, he'd been in an awful hurry to get out to the platform and this was the only train there.

After boarding, Betsy cautiously made her way down the length of the cars. She spotted him in the next to last carriage. Holding a bundle on his lap, he sat in the seat closest to the window, his nose buried in a newspaper.

Betsy smiled as she took a seat not far away. Now that she knew where he was, keeping him in her sights should be easy.

"What kind of deal?" Mrs. Jeffries prodded.

"That's the funny part," Mrs. Goodge said eagerly. "Arthur Grant doesn't have any money, so he couldn't be doin' any buyin'."

"Maybe he was selling one," the housekeeper suggested.

"He doesn't own any of 'em," the cook replied promptly. "I found that out when I was checkin' with my sources about the family in general. There's a valuable art collection, all right," she continued, "but it belongs to Neville Grant. None of it belongs to his son."

"His mother didn't leave him anything?"

"Nothing." Mrs. Goodge pursed her lips. "Not so much as a picture frame. She didn't share her husband's passion for art. As a matter of fact, she and Neville Grant were reported to be at odds over his spending the family money on buying paintings. One of the rumors I heard claimed that they was squabblin' about it so much that if Arthur's mother hadn't up and died when she did, Neville was goin' to divorce her."

" 'Ello, 'ello," a singsong voice cried from down the hall. "Are you in there, Mrs. Goodge? It's me, Gavin. I've got a delivery for ya."

The cook brightened immediately and leapt to her feet. "Come on in, lad," she cried, lunging for the kettle and snatching it up. "It's the grocer's boy," she hissed at the housekeeper as she plopped the kettle on the burner. "He's always got heaps of gossip."

Mrs. Jeffries nodded and got up. "I'll leave you to it," she murmured as a young man carrying a huge covered wicker basket lumbered into the kitchen. She smiled at him and left.

As she climbed the back stairs to her room, Mrs. Jeffries began going over precisely what they'd learned so far. But it was still most confusing.

By the time she reached her room she was almost convinced that it was the most convoluted case they'd ever had. She walked over and sat down in her chair next to the window. Staring blindly out the window, she let her mind go blank. That was a neat trick she'd picked up over the past few years. Sometimes she did her best thinking by not thinking at all. She kept staring out at the rooftops of London, letting her brain leap willy-nilly where it would. Ideas, thoughts, unrelated bits of information — it all whirled about in her head in a rush of nonsense. But Mrs. Jeffries wasn't overly concerned. She'd sort the pieces out later. Right now, all she was really concerned with was a pattern, a connection of some kind. There was always a common thread in every case they'd had. It was like having a hundred keys to unlock one door. Difficult, yes, but not impossible. Especially if one had learned to pay attention to the kind of lock on the door. That's what she did now — tried to find what kind of lock this door had.

Smythe stood under the TO LET sign of the empty building on busy Villiers Street. He wondered why Blimpey had sent a street Arab to tell him to meet him here instead of at the pub. The street was quite busy with hansoms, pedestrians and shopkeepers all trying to get about their business. Smythe pulled out his watch, noted the time and then glanced at the facade of Gattis Restaurant across from where he stood. He blinked, amazed, as Blimpey Groggins, no cleaner than he ever was, emerged from the front door.

Blimpey spotted him immediately. Lifting his arm, he waved, motioning him over.

"Eat 'ere regularly, do ya?" Smythe asked. Gattis was one of London's most elegant restaurants. Smythe had the money to buy the place, but actually setting foot in it as a customer would never occur to him. He didn't like to think he'd be intimidated by a bunch of toffs — he wouldn't. Well, not too intimidated. But he couldn't for the life of him think of what Blimpey Groggins, disheveled and dirty, was doing here.

215

Blimpey laughed. "Not hardly, mate. Just was inside havin' a chat with one of the staff. The maître d' here owes me a couple of favors and I was collectin'."

Smythe wondered what kind of favors Blimpey was cashing in, but didn't like to ask. Sometimes it didn't pay to be too curious about someone like Groggins. "How come you wanted me to meet ya 'ere?"

"I'm a bit pressed for time today," Blimpey replied. He jerked his head toward the end of the road. "There's a decent pub down there. Let's have a quick one. I do my best talkin' over a glass."

Smythe eyed his companion speculatively as they headed off. "You weren't too busy to get my information, were ya?" the coachman asked.

"Don't be daft," Blimpey said. "Have I ever failed ya?" They were abreast of the pub now. He reached out and yanked open the door. "Trust me, Smythe. Trust me. I might be busy, but that don't mean I'm not giving ya good service."

"The best that money can buy." Smythe stepped past his companion and into the pub. He was relieved to see it was an ordinary, plain sort of place with benches and tables and a bored-looking publican behind the bar. "Two bitters," he ordered quickly, knowing that the sooner he got beer pouring down Blimpey's throat, the faster he'd get his information.

A few minutes later, they were seated at a table. Blimpey took a long sip from his glass and then gave a loud, satisfied sigh. "Ah. That's good."

"Now that you've wet yer whistle," Smythe said, "what did ya learn?"

"You're an impatient sort, Smythe," Blimpey commented. "You ought to slow down a bit, take time to sniff the air and enjoy yerself. But seein' as we're both in a bit of a hurry today, I'll get right to it." His expression sobered. "It ain't very pretty. But ya know that already. The woman that Mordecai's boys was paid to kill is named Irene Simmons. She's an artist's model."

"I thought that might be 'er." Smythe kept his face impassive. "She's disappeared."

"But I bet no one's found her body, 'ave they?" Blimpey replied. "Like I told ya yesterday, it went wrong. They didn't do it. Mordecai himself is rumored to be havin' a fit, thinkin' his good name's been ruined."

"Why'd it go wrong? Were ya able to find out?" Smythe decided that getting as many details as possible just might help them track down Irene Simmons, especially as it looked like she hadn't been murdered — at least not by this particular set of hired killers.

"Story I got — and I've no doubt it's true" — Blimpey took a quick drink — "is that two of Mordecai's boys was going to be waiting for the woman when she walked down the street."

"You mean they was just standing on the street, waiting for 'er?" Smythe didn't think so, not in that neighborhood. "That can't be right.

She disappeared from a posh area. Thugs like Mordecai's scum woulda stuck out like a sore thumb. Someone woulda spotted 'em and called the police."

"They weren't just standin' on the street," Blimpey corrected. "They was waiting at the top of the mews. It connects with Beltrane Gardens a half a dozen houses down from where this woman was supposed to be goin'. Anyway, as I was sayin', they was to grab her as she was walkin' toward Holland Park Road."

"She was supposed to be goin' to the Grant house," Smythe said. "The same 'ouse where Underhill 'imself got murdered a week later."

"I know." Blimpey grinned. "Knowin' things is me business, remember. Now do ya want to hear the rest of it or not?"

"Go on," Smythe said irritably.

"Anyways, like I was sayin', the thugs was to grab her when she reached the mouth of the alley. But she never got to 'em," Blimpey explained. "They waited and waited and waited, but she never come."

"Do they know for sure she went into the Grant house?" Smythe asked. He wanted to make good and sure that these thugs, who apparently weren't the smartest lads about, actually knew what they were on about.

"Oh, yes," Blimpey affirmed. "They had their eyes on 'er from the time she got off the omnibus and walked up Holland Park Road. She walked with a woman as far as Beltrane Gardens and then continued on by herself to the Grant house. It was at that point, after she was almost there, that they took off for the mouth of the mews and tucked themselves back out of sight. Like ya said, Mordecai's boys would stick out right smart in a posh neighborhood like that. They couldn't afford to be seen by too many people."

"Maybe the girl did spot them," Smythe suggested. "Maybe she came out of the house and went in another direction?"

"There isn't any other way," Blimpey said. "Not unlessin' yer goin' through someone's back garden, and I don't think a young woman would be up to that. Besides, if that were the case, why didn't she go on home or go to the police?"

He had a point, Smythe conceded silently. "Do these thugs 'ave any idea what 'appened?" he asked. "A woman doesn't just disappear into thin air."

"They figure she either never left the Grant house," Blimpey said, "or that she got nabbed before she reached the mouth of the mews."

"They see anything?"

"One of 'em claimed there was a carriage pulled up in front of the house." Blimpey shrugged. "But that don't mean much. It was gettin' toward evening and there was a lot of traffic. A neighborhood like that would have plenty of carriages and hansoms goin' in and out."

"So no one really knows what happened."

"All they know is what didn't happen."

"Do you believe yer sources are tellin' the

219

truth?" Smythe motioned impatiently with his hand. "No, that's not what I mean. Do ya think that Mordecai's boys is tellin' the truth? Now that Underhill is dead, could be they just want to put the word out that they didn't kill someone for 'im."

"It's the truth all right." Blimpey shook his head vehemently. "Underhill was furious with Mordecai for botching the murder. They had a blazin' row about it the next day. Underhill, stupid bugger, wanted his money back. Mordecai said he didn't give refunds and told him he'd get the job done as soon as they could find the girl. That's the strange part — they can't find her either. She's plum disappeared."

Smythe's brows drew together in an ominous frown. "They're not still lookin' for 'er, are they?"

"Nah. Mordecai don't take *that* much pride in his work. With Underhill dead, he's not goin' to care one way or another about Irene Simmons. The girl means nothing to him."

Smythe leaned forward, his expression grim. "I wonder if Mordecai murdered Underhill."

Blimpey laughed again. "With poison? Not bloody likely. He wouldn't be that neat about it. When scum like him do their work, they don't bother to be tidy. Besides, why would he want Underhill dead? He was a customer."

"I see yer point," Smythe muttered. "But it don't make sense."

"Who says life has to make sense?" Blimpey

shrugged philosophically. "All I know is she didn't get carved up by Mordecai's thugs and she ain't been heard from since."

"So she's either still in the house," Smythe mused, "or she was kidnapped before she reached the mews."

"Or she was grabbed right before she went into the house," Blimpey corrected. "The thugs took off just as they saw her reaching the Grant house. They didn't see her go inside."

"I wonder what kind of a carriage it was?" he murmured, remembering what Betsy had told them.

"I don't know and I ain't sure I can find out. Mordecai's thugs don't usually talk to the likes of me." Blimpey belched softly. "Get me another, will ya? Then I'll tell ya the rest of it."

"Rest of it?" Smythe half rose and waved at the barman, gesturing for another round when he had the man's attention. "You mean there's more?"

"Course there's more," Blimpey bragged. "I always give ya yer money's worth."

Betsy's lungs hurt as she hurried to keep her quarry in sight. He'd gotten off the train at Reigate and she, keeping well behind him, had followed suit.

But he must have been feeling quite confident he wasn't being followed, because he never once looked over his shoulder as he left the station. Since leaving the town proper, Betsy had trailed him a good half mile now, first down a country lane and then onto a footpath through a copse of trees. The trees grew close enough together that she couldn't see all that far ahead, but she could still hear his footsteps echoing in front of her.

She stumbled over a tree root snaking across the foot path, righted herself and plunged onward, scrambling none too delicately toward a point ahead where the trees had started to thin. She stopped suddenly as she realized she couldn't hear his footfalls against the path. Her heart pounded in her ears. Her breathing sounded loud enough to wake the dead as she stood still and listened. A moment later, she heard him start to move.

Betsy's whole body sagged in relief. She'd feel a right fool if he'd suddenly turned tail and come back this way. She'd feel even more foolish if it turned out he wasn't leading her anywhere except his own home.

"Maybe someone was playing a joke on your coachman," Barnes said softly. He and the inspector were back at the Grant house, waiting in the living room while the butler went to fetch Arthur Grant. The inspector had just told the constable the disturbing information he'd learned from Smythe.

"That's certainly possible, I suppose," Witherspoon replied. He kept one eye on the entrance to the drawing room. "But Smythe seemed quite convinced the man was sincere. True or not, though, we must investigate it."

"Too bad it's Mordecai." Barnes grimaced. "None of his lot will ever turn on him. Too many that've tried are dead."

"Well, we can't prosecute on rumors," Witherspoon said dejectedly, "but on the other hand, according to what Smythe was told, this young woman wasn't murdered."

"But she's still missin'." Barnes didn't like that. He didn't like it one bit. Unlike the inspector, he wasn't too sure that Mordecai's boys had failed in their mission. As a gang leader, Mordecai wasn't quite as stupid as some of the others operating out of the east end or the docks. The constable wouldn't put it past the thug to put the word out that they'd failed when in reality, there was some poor woman at the bottom of the Thames trussed up like a Christmas goose.

"The butler said you wanted to see me," Arthur Grant said as he entered the drawing room. "I can't think why. I've already told you everything I know about this dreadful business." He stalked across the room and came to a halt right in front of Witherspoon.

The inspector noticed the man's face was haggard and thin, his pale complexion now almost a dead white, and there was a decided twitch in his right eye. "I'm afraid we've a few more questions we must ask you," he told him.

"Questions? That's ridiculous. What else could I tell you?"

"Where did Mr. Underhill conduct his business?" Witherspoon asked, thinking he might have to be careful in how he broached this interview. Arthur Grant looked as though he might faint.

"Conduct his business?" Arthur stammered. "I'm afraid I don't understand the question."

"He couldn't have done business out of his lodgings, sir," the inspector explained. "When his premises were searched there weren't any invoices or records or ledgers or anything at all to support the notion that he made his living as an artists' agent or broker."

Arthur stepped back a pace. "Why are you asking me? I didn't have anything to do with Underhill's business. His coming round here on the day he died was purely a social call. We were social acquaintances, nothing more. I know nothing of his business affairs, absolutely nothing." As he spoke he stepped farther and farther away from the two policemen.

"I'm afraid that's not true, sir," Witherspoon said, his gaze shifting slightly to one side as he spied Neville and Mary Grant standing in the drawing room door. "We know for a fact that you were doing business with Mr. Underhill. That's the reason you invited him here that day. Have you ever been to Mr. Underhill's lodgings?"

Grant hesitated briefly. "Only once."

"When was that, sir?" Barnes asked, looking up from his notebook.

"A few months ago." Arthur's eye spasmed furiously. "I went round for tea one afternoon. James had some new paintings he wanted to show me."

"Only once, sir?" Witherspoon shook his head. "Are you sure?"

"Of course I'm sure," Arthur insisted, his voice rising shrilly. "Why shouldn't I be sure?"

"Have you been there since Mr. Underhill was murdered?" Barnes asked calmly.

"No," Arthur cried. "Absolutely not. Who told you I was there? If it was that pie-faced old hag of a landlady of his, she's lying."

"But she isn't lying, sir," Witherspoon said mildly. "Why would she? She's no reason to tell us anything except the truth. Now, why don't you tell the constable and I why you claimed to be a policeman and then spent the afternoon searching James Underhill's lodgings? What were you looking for?"

"Nothing," he blurted out. Then he clamped his hand over his mouth. "I wasn't looking for anything."

"But you admit you were there?"

"I'm not sure," Arthur wailed. "Maybe I was. I don't know. I'm confused."

"Should we bring the landlady here to identify him, sir?" Barnes asked the inspector.

Arthur looked from one policeman to the other, his expression frantic. He still hadn't noticed his father standing behind him. "You don't have to do that. All right, I'll admit it. I was there. I did tell her I was a policeman. But that's all I did. I didn't kill him."

"Then what were you looking for, sir?" the inspector pressed. "Why would an innocent man go to a dead man's lodgings under false pretenses unless he had something to hide? What were you looking for that day, sir?"

"I don't know," Arthur cried passionately. "He told me he hadn't kept them in his rooms but I didn't believe him. Then when I saw he'd been telling the truth, that they weren't there, you see, I knew they had to be somewhere. I knew I had to find them. I've got to find them. So I thought there might be a key. If I don't, I'm ruined. Absolutely ruined."

Neville stepped into the room, for once not thumping his cane loud enough to rattle the windows. But his son wasn't aware of his father's entrance. Arthur's gaze was focused on the two policemen in front of him.

"Ruined, sir?" Barnes said gently. "In what way? Why don't you just tell us the truth, sir? It'll go easier on you in the long run."

Arthur blanched at the constable's comment. "I didn't kill him," he screamed. "I didn't kill him. I don't care what anyone says. I didn't do it. I was going to pay him what he wanted. I had the money. I'd borrowed it from Aunt Helen."

"For God's sake, boy, shut up!" Neville thundered, poking his son in the back with his cane. "Don't say another word."

Arthur let out a squawk and whirled around. "Father? You've got to believe me. I didn't do it."

"Shut up!" Neville banged his cane against the floor. "Do you hear me, boy? Be quiet." He looked at the inspector. "Are you arresting my son?"

Witherspoon was quite taken aback. All he'd planned on doing was asking a few questions. "No. But we would like to ask him some more questions."

Neville stared at the policeman speculatively, as though he was weighing his choices. "Does he have to answer them?"

"Your son cannot be forced to answer our questions," the inspector replied. He'd no idea why the Grants were reacting like this, but both the father and the son now appeared almost frantic with worry. Witherspoon couldn't readily see that he had any evidence to connect them to Underhill's murder, but considering their suspicious behaviour, he decided to carry on. "However, we can ask him to accompany us to the station to help us with our inquiries."

Everyone in the room knew what that meant. Arthur would, in fact, end up under arrest.

"I see." Neville flashed a quick look at his son. "Tell them the truth, boy. Tell them now."

"The truth?" Arthur's voice shook. "I've no idea what you're talking about, Father . . ."

"Arthur, don't be such an imbecile," Neville snapped. He gestured at Witherspoon and Barnes. "They already know you were cooking up some silly scheme with Underhill. Now go ahead and tell them what it was so they'll go away and leave us in peace. Whatever it was you were planning can't be nearly as serious as a murder charge."

Arthur's mouth opened and closed, as though he were trying to speak, but no words came out.

Betsy dodged behind a tree and stared at the clearing. Two hundred feet ahead she watched the man she'd been following disappear through the door of a cottage — quite a large cottage, double storied and possibly with an attic on top, but nevertheless a cottage. A wooden fence, boards missing in spots, encircled an overgrown garden. The lawn was tufted with tiny hillocks, weeds sprouted in the flower beds and the stone walkway was cracked in several places.

The outside had once been white but was now a dull, dismal gray. Shutters, one of them hanging askew, banked the windows on either side of the door. No smoke came out of either of the chimney pots on the roof.

Betsy's heart thumped against her chest as she tried to decide what to do. Walking boldly up to the door and demanding entrance might not be too smart, she thought, casting a quick glance around at the surroundings. This place was all by itself out in the middle of nowhere. If the man got stroppy, she might be in trouble. Goodness knows, she'd not passed another living soul for a good half hour, so if she got in trouble, screaming her head off wouldn't do any good.

But she had a feeling about this place. Following the man from the gallery had been a risk, but now that she was here, she was almost certain she was on to something important. But what to do about it? Betsy surveyed the area. The clearing was a good two hundred feet long and at least that much wide. She couldn't sneak up to the house from the front, but maybe there would be a bit more shelter from the back.

Betsy moved quietly from tree to tree, making her way around the house and keeping her eyes peeled to make sure she wasn't seen. When she found herself standing directly in line with the corner of the house, she decided to move closer. The trees were thinning off up the hillside, useless as hiding places. Taking a deep breath, she lifted the hem of her skirt and dashed across the clearing toward the side of the house.

Reaching it, she flattened herself against the wood and took a long, deep breath of air into her lungs. Along the side, there were two more windows. Both of them were shut, but even from where she stood, she could see that the curtains on the one closest to where she stood were wide open.

Betsy eased away from the building and edged closer to the window. She kept her head cocked to one side, listening hard for the sound of voices. Her foot hit a patch of mud and made an ugly squishing sound as she crept down the side.

Finally, she reached the window. She bent her knees and ducked down so that her head was under the sill. Slowly, carefully, Betsy raised up until she could see over the edge.

Her eyes widened and her heartbeat quickened. She'd been right to follow him. She'd been right all along. It had been a kidnapping and the proof of it was right in front of her.

Irene Simmons. A young, dark-haired woman sat less than five feet from where she stood. Betsy was sure it was her. The description they had of Irene matched this woman completely.

What to do now?

Through the window, Betsy heard the telltale squeak of a door opening. Then footsteps as someone came into the captive's room.

Betsy pulled back out of view, flattening herself against the wall. What was she going to do? She had to do something. That poor woman was at the mercy of some fiend.

Holding her breath, she took another quick peek. Her mouth gaped open in surprise at what she saw.

Irene Simmons, kidnap victim, appeared to be locked in a passionate embrace with a tall, dark-haired man. Irene wasn't resisting the man. As a matter of fact, from where Betsy stood, it looked as if the girl was participating wholeheartedly.

"Well, I never," Betsy mumbled. She started to back away, thinking she'd got everything completely wrong. Mainly, she was concerned that the woman in the house wasn't Irene, but some perfectly innocent lady giving her husband a perfectly natural embrace. Retreating backward and shaking her head in disgust at her own stupidity,

Betsy didn't see the man step out from the side of the house. She stumbled into him. Whirling around, she found herself face to face with the fellow she'd trailed from the St. James gallery. "Oh no," she cried. "Look, there's a good explanation . . ."

He grabbed her arm and yanked her towards him. "I told you to leave us alone," he snarled. "But no, you had to follow me, had to keep sticking your pretty little nose in where it weren't wanted." He pulled her toward a door at the back of the house.

"Let me go." Betsy tried to jerk her arm free, but he held on fast. "I told you, there's a good explanation . . ."

"I'll bet there is," he said.

The back door flew open and the dark-haired man came out. The woman, her eyes wide with fear, was right behind him. "George? What's going on?" he asked. His voice was tinged with a faint accent.

"This is the girl I told you about," George said, tugging Betsy forward none too gently. "The one who came round asking all those questions yesterday. She must have followed me. We'd better bring her inside, quickly." He started for the door as the other two stepped back a pace. "I don't know if she brought any of Underhill's thugs with her."

Betsy dug her heels into the ground and resisted with all her might. "No one followed me," she said before she could stop herself. She looked at the woman standing behind the dark-haired man. "Are you Irene Simmons?"

"Why, yes," she replied.

"We'll ask the questions," the man holding her arm said. He tried tugging her forward again.

Betsy had had it. This man talked like a thug, but he wasn't really very good at it. For starters, now that they'd stopped, she could feel his hand trembling as he hung onto her. She yanked her arm out of his grasp, made a fist with her other hand and cuffed him smartly on the shoulder.

"Ow," he yelped.

"Keep your hands off me, you silly fool," she ordered. She put her hands on her hips and looked directly at the woman. "You'd better listen. Nanette Lanier sent me."

"Nanette." The woman's eyes widened.

"Be careful, darling," the dark-haired man warned. "It might be a trick."

"Oh, for goodness' sake," Betsy grumbled. Now that she'd had a moment to calm down, she'd decided these three were the least likely looking bunch of hoodlums she'd ever seen. The one called George was shaking in his boots, Irene was pale with fear and even the dark-haired man, the calmest of the lot, was wide-eyed and anxious with worry. They weren't going to hurt her. "Let's go inside and talk like civilized people. We're not going to settle a ruddy thing standing out here."

"I'm afraid we're going to have to search your

rooms, Mr. Grant," Witherspoon told the trembling young man. "If needed, I'm sure we can get a warrant."

"You've already searched the house once," Neville complained.

"It was only a cursory search, sir," Witherspoon said. "Do I have your permission to search your son's rooms again, or shall I get a warrant?" He held his breath and tried to remember what the judge's Rules said about a situation like this.

"That won't be necessary," Neville Grant said. "Go ahead and search. You won't find anything. My boy may be a fool but he's not a killer."

"Really, Neville," Mary snapped. "This is intolerable. We will not be treated like common criminals."

"I'm only trying to get at the truth, ma'am," the inspector said.

Mary Grant ignored him. From the expression on her face as she glared at her husband, she was more furious at him than she was at the inspector. "I won't have policemen stomping through my home. I demand that you send for our solicitor at once."

"Why?" Neville asked. "Arthur's got nothing to hide. He didn't kill James Underhill. Why should he? Now go ahead, boy, tell the inspector what kind of silly scheme you were cooking up with Underhill so we can have some peace in this house."

"Arthur, don't say a word," Mary ordered. "If your father won't do anything to protect you, I'll send for our solicitor myself."

"I know how to take care of my son. Stay out of this, Mary," Neville commanded. "Arthur's got no reason not to talk to the police. Now go on, boy, tell them the truth."

Mary stared at her husband and her stepson with an expression of utter contempt on her face. Without saying another word, she turned on her heel and stalked out.

Arthur moaned softly. "I didn't mean to do it, Father, but I was short of money and they were going to toss me out of the club if I didn't pay up my gambling debts."

Neville drew back a bit. "What didn't you mean to do?"

Arthur swallowed hard. "I meant to get them back," he said softly. "I really did. James promised he wouldn't sell them. He'd bought them for himself, you see. He'd come into some money so he wanted them for himself. But then you were going to sell them and that American, well, they act like they're so friendly, but really they're quite a suspicious bunch, aren't they? Well, he insisted they be authenticated. I couldn't let that happen, could I? I mean, they're good forgeries but an expert could tell in an instant they weren't the real thing."

Neville Grant had gone utterly pale.

"Forgeries," Witherspoon said. He cast a quick, worried glance at the old man. Fellow didn't look well. "Precisely what forgeries are you referring to?"

"Well." Arthur tried a sickly smile. "I mean, it wasn't really a forgery. Like I said, I was going to buy them back. James promised I could, you know. He kept them out at his country cottage. He promised he'd send for them. I thought they might be at his lodgings, but they weren't there and they're not at the cottage either. But they must be somewhere."

"What are you talking about, boy?" Grant whispered. "Which paintings did you have forged?"

Arthur looked surprised by the question. "Oh, didn't I say? The Caldararos, of course."

Neville's mouth opened and closed. He jerked spasmodically, clutched at his heart and collapsed. He'd have fallen flat on his face if the inspector and Barnes hadn't grabbed him.

Chapter 10

"I'm sure Betsy will be here any moment now," Mrs. Jeffries said with a calmness she didn't feel. She glanced at the anxious faces around the table and forced herself to smile reassuringly. It was almost nine. Dinner had come and gone. Everyone was gathered back at Upper Edmonton Gardens for their meeting and Betsy wasn't home.

Smythe had gone beyond being worried. He'd stopped pacing the floor and ranting and raving a good half hour ago. Now he just sat staring at the carriage clock on the cupboard, almost as though he were willing time to stop. "When's the inspector due?" he asked.

"I don't know," Mrs. Jeffries replied. "He didn't come home for dinner and as he hasn't sent a message, I can only assume that means he's tied up on this case."

Smythe got to his feet. He knew what he had to do. "I'm going to find him. He can get every copper in London lookin' for 'er." It was either do that or slowly go insane.

Everyone looked at Mrs. Jeffries. They were all

worried but no one was really sure that bringing the inspector in at this point was such a good idea.

"Give her a bit more time, Smythe," Hatchet said conversationally, though he was distraught as well. "Miss Betsy is a highly intelligent and most capable young woman. I'm sure nothing has happened to her."

"But what if somethin' 'as?" Smythe shook his head vehemently. "What if she's been 'urt or . . . or . . ." He stopped, unable to put his greatest fear into words.

"She's not been hurt and she ain't dead," Luty declared confidently. She hated seeing the pain on her friend's face, but she knew that if she sympathized the least little bit, he'd fall to pieces. "Betsy's on the hunt and she's just fine. Why, if she was a man, we'd not think a thing of her bein' a few hours late like this. There's been times when you and Wiggins have been out half the night and worryin' the rest of us sick. We didn't go runnin' to the inspector." But they'd been tempted to, Luty remembered.

Smythe closed his eyes briefly and clenched his hands into fists. "All right. I'll give it another 'alf 'our . . ."

"I don't think you'll 'ave to," Wiggins said. He'd wandered over to the far side of the kitchen and was peeking out the window that looked out onto the road. "There's a carriage pulling up outside and . . ." He stood on tiptoe to get a closer look. "Cor blimey, it's her. It's Betsy, and she's got three other people with her."

"Go let them in the front door," Mrs. Jeffries ordered the footman. "The inspector's not home and it'll save them coming around to the back." It would also give the coachman a few moments to get his emotions under control.

Wiggins raced off to do as he was bid.

Mrs. Goodge got up and turned her back on the others as she headed for the sink. "I'll put the kettle on," she mumbled, hoping that no one would notice the tears of relief that were running down her cheeks. "I think we could all do with a cup of tea."

"I think you'd better have a look at this." Barnes motioned the inspector into the bedroom. "We found it under the mattress." He held a small glass vial between his fingers. "Have a whiff, sir."

The inspector took a deep breath. The scent of bitter almonds drifted up his nostrils. "Oh, dear. We'd better send this along to Dr. Bosworth to be analyzed," he said. "But I've no doubt what it is."

Barnes put the stopper back inside. "Stupid of him to keep it under his mattress. Why didn't he get rid of it?"

"That's a bit more difficult to do than one might think," Witherspoon said. But the constable had made a valid point. Why hadn't Arthur gotten rid of the damaging evidence? The man wasn't the brightest chap, of course. But he wasn't a complete half-wit, either. "Perhaps he meant to but hadn't gotten around to it yet."

"Yes, sir. But leaving cyanide under your mattress" — Barnes put the vial in his pocket — "that really is idiotic, sir. Almost deliberately so, if you know what I mean. Are we going to arrest him now?"

"I'm afraid I'm going to have to." Witherspoon sighed. "Pity about his father. But let's keep our fingers crossed that Mr. Grant will be all right. Is the doctor still with him?"

"Yes." Barnes nodded. "When I poked my head in a few minutes ago, Mr. Grant had regained consciousness."

"Oh, dear." Witherspoon was in a quandry. "I didn't mean that the way it sounded. Of course I'm glad the elder Mr. Grant is conscious, but now I'm not sure what we ought to do. It would be so much easier to arrest Arthur if his father were asleep. I don't want to risk the poor old chap having another attack or fit or whatever it was he had."

"Well, sir, that can't be helped. Arthur's admitted to conspiring with Underhill. Forgery is a felony, sir. With the physical evidence of the cyanide, we've no choice but to arrest him."

"That's true," Witherspoon mused. "But conspiring in a forgery is a far cry from murder. Besides, if what Arthur says is true, why would he kill Underhill? He needed him alive. Underhill appears to be the only one who knows where the genuine Caldararos might be."

"We've already dispatched a telegram to Kent, sir," Barnes pointed out. "Maybe the local police will find them when they search Underhill's cottage."

"Let's hope so, Constable." Witherspoon sighed. "For some reason, I've a feeling those missing paintings are important to this case. But I can't quite determine precisely how."

"You'll suss it out in the end, sir," Barnes said. "Should I go and get young Mr. Grant now?"

Witherspoon hesitated. Drat. "He's upstairs in his father's room, isn't he?"

"Both he and Mrs. Grant are at Mr. Grant's bedside."

"Then we'll wait until tomorrow morning to arrest him. I won't run the risk. My conscience would torment me if in arresting Arthur we inadvertently harmed his father. We'll leave a constable on duty here and come back tomorrow morning. Perhaps the elder Mr. Grant will be stronger then and more able to cope."

"What if Arthur tries to scarper?"

"I don't think Arthur will be going anywhere," Witherspoon replied. "He's far too nervous a disposition to try making a run for it."

Barnes stared at his superior for a moment, his expression speculative. "You don't think he's guilty, do you, sir?"

The inspector smiled faintly. "You're very perceptive, Constable. And also quite correct. I don't think the fellow murdered anyone."

Witherspoon couldn't explain it, even to himself. But he had a feeling the young man wasn't a killer. "I know the evidence looks bad, but I can't quite see him doing the planning it would take to kill James Underhill with poisoned mints. Frankly, he seems far too much a bumbler."

"It could be an act, sir," Barnes suggested. "Perhaps he's not quite the fool everyone thinks."

"Well, his father seems to think him a fool," the inspector pointed out. "And he ought to know."

Every female in the room was staring at Alex Morante, as he asked to be addressed, like they'd never seen a man before. All right, Smythe thought, so he's not a bad-lookin' bloke. Even Mrs. Jeffries, who ought to have known better, was hanging on the fellow's every word. Just because Morante was as handsome as the devil and had courage and bravery oozing from his pores, the women were all atwitter over him. Smythe hated him. He glanced at Hatchet and Wiggins. They looked like they hated him too.

"I kidnapped Irene to save her life," Morante claimed.

"That's right. He did," Irene added. She gave him an adoring smile. "If it wasn't for Alex, I'd be dead. James Underhill had hired people to kill me. They were going to kidnap me that night."

"But instead 'e kidnapped you?" Wiggins jerked his head toward the Spaniard.

"I'm afraid I don't quite understand," Mrs.

Jeffries said. She looked at the artist. "How did you know that Underhill was going to harm Miss Simmons?"

"Irene had come by my studio about two weeks ago. She was posing for me," he explained. "I'd sent her into the next room to put an apron on over her dress when Underhill stormed into my studio. He demanded I forge a painting for him — a Caravaggio, to be precise. He had a client who wanted a forgery to foist off on some banker as collateral for a loan. I told him I didn't do that sort of thing . . ."

"Why would Underhill want you to do it, then?" Smythe asked. "I mean, did he pick yer name out of a hat or somethin'?"

"Smythe," Betsy hissed. "Don't be so rude."

"No, it's a fair question." Alex held up his hand. "He asked me to do it because I'd done it before. I'd forged three Caldararos last year — but I thought they were to be known as copies only. I didn't know he was going to foist them off as the real thing. When I found out what he'd done, I was furious."

"How did you find out?" Mrs. Jeffries asked.

"Underhill told me." Alex smiled bitterly. "The man had no shame. He admitted what he'd done. After I'd painted the Caldararos, I started hearing rumors about him, about some of the scams he pulled on his clients and on the artists he dealt with."

"So you started askin' questions?" Wiggins guessed.

"That's right." Alex shrugged. "And I didn't like the answers I got. I'm not a saint, but I'm not a criminal."

"All right, go on with yer tale now," Luty commanded. "Underhill arrived at yer studio. Then what happened?"

"When I told him to leave, told him I wasn't interested, he got angry. He told me I'd no choice, that I had to forge the Caravaggio or I'd be sorry." Alex raised one eyebrow. "I don't like being threatened. I told him to get out and said if he came back I'd go to the police. But he laughed at me and said that I couldn't, that I was the one who had actually done the forging. If I told the police what he'd done, I'd be arrested. It would be my word against his. He was from an old, respectable family and I was a foreigner. Who would the police believe? Him or me?" His mouth curved in a cynical smile. "Underhill made his point and then he left. But I'd forgotten about Irene. She came back into the room and she was as pale as a ghost. I knew she'd overheard everything. She was scared and I don't blame her. She told me she couldn't pose, grabbed her shawl and ran out."

"So how did Underhill know she was there?" Wiggins asked.

"I ran after her. Underhill was waving down a hansom and saw her leaving my studio. He guessed that she'd overheard everything," Alex said. "I hoped everything would be all right, that Underhill wouldn't do anything. But then a few

243

days later, I heard a rumor that someone had hired some thugs to kill Irene."

"It wasn't a rumor," Smythe said.

"But why?" Mrs. Goodge asked. "I mean, why murder just Irene?" She pointed at the Spaniard. "You knew what he was up to. You could ruin him just as easily. Why just kill the one of you?"

"But I couldn't tell," Morante explained. "Not without ruining myself. Even if the police believed I'd been duped into doing those forgeries, my career as an artist would be ruined. No respectable gallery or broker would handle my work. Underhill knew his secret was safe with me, but he didn't want Irene knowing it. So he was determined to silence her."

"How'd you find out about the bogus note that Underhill sent to Irene luring her to the Grant house?" Luty asked.

"I knew I had to do something to protect her," he said. "So I did the only thing I could. I went to Underhill's lodgings. I told him I'd changed my mind about doing the forgery. I told him I was broke and needed the money."

"And he believed you?" Hatchet asked.

"Oh, yes." Morante smiled cynically. "I can be quite convincing. I demanded some cash immediately, a kind of down payment on the forgery. I knew that he kept his money in the bedroom and I wanted a chance to search his desk. When he went to get the cash, I had a quick look. The note he'd written to Irene, the one luring her to the Grant house, was on his desk."

"Just sittin' there right where you could see it?" Smythe's tone was disbelieving.

"No," Morante replied. "I had to hunt for it. It was under a telegram Underhill was sending to someone in Kent. But as soon as I saw the note, I knew what he was planning. Why else would he have someone else's stationery in his desk? I made a note of the time of the appointment and the address, waited till Underhill came back into the room, took his money and left." His dark eyes sparkled with amusement. "I used Underhill's own money to rent the house in the country."

"The place he took me to be safe," Irene said, giving him a warm smile.

"Then what happened?" Luty asked.

"I knew that Irene would be going to Beltrane Gardens at six o'clock on the eighth." He nodded at his friend, who'd sat quietly through the entire narrative. "With George's help, we managed to foil the murder."

"George lent us the carriage." Irene flashed a grateful smile at George, who blushed a fiery red.

"That's right," Morante agreed. "George lent me his brougham . . ."

"It's an old one," George put in. "It used to belong to my father. But he's dead so he doesn't drive it anymore."

"Then what happened?" Hatchet asked.

"Then we waited outside the Grant house. I spotted a couple of thugs at the mouth of the

245

mews so I knew we'd better grab her before she went inside." He smiled apologetically at Irene. "When she started up the walk, I called her. She turned, recognized me and came towards the carriage. Before she knew what happened, I pulled her inside and George took off."

"Why didn't you scream?" Mrs. Goodge demanded.

"I couldn't. Alex put his hand over my mouth." She didn't look as though she were still annoyed at Alex. "By the time we were on our way out of London, Alex had convinced me of the terrible danger I was in. I didn't know what to do. I couldn't get a message to my grandma, and I didn't dare send one to Nanette. Underhill and Nanette have some kind of relationship, and Alex wasn't sure we could trust her."

"But yer poor old granny was worried sick about you," Luty groused. "What if she'd needed something? What if she'd gotten sick . . ."

"We took care of that," Irene said quickly. "Alex slipped into the flat and refilled her medicine bottle when she was asleep. Besides that, George has kept an eye on her."

"Why didn't you come back when Underhill was murdered?" Hatchet asked.

"We didn't know if it was safe." Alex shrugged. "We knew he'd paid to have her murdered, but not being familiar with that sort of thing, we weren't sure if whoever had taken his money would still feel he had to do it."

"It took me quite a bit of talking to convince

them it was safe to come here," Betsy said. She looked pointedly at Smythe. "That's one of the reasons we was so late."

"What do you know about Underhill's killin'?" Smythe asked them bluntly.

All three of them looked surprised by the question.

"What could we possibly know about it?" Alex asked. "We were in the country when he was killed."

"Yeah, but you've admitted you were in 'is flat. If ya knew Underhill at all, ya knew he was always chewin' them mints. It woulda been dead easy for ya to pop a tampered tin of mints into the man's coat pocket and then sit back and wait for yer problem to be solved permanently."

Morante stared at Smythe for a moment, then flicked a quick speculative glance at Betsy. He grinned. "Agreed. I could have done that. But" — he looked the coachman dead in the eye — "I didn't. I'm not a murderer. If that had been my solution, I wouldn't have gone to all the trouble of kidnapping Irene, involving my friend and hiding out in the country. I would have simply killed him the day I went to his lodgings."

The two men stared at one another, taking each other's measure. Smythe leaned back and folded his arms across his massive chest. "I reckon there's some merit to what you're sayin'."

"So what do we do now?" Irene asked.

"I suggest you all go home," Mrs. Jeffries said calmly. She looked at Irene. "I'm sure Nanette will be delighted to see that you're alive and well."

As soon as they were gone, Betsy turned to the others. "I'm ever so sorry I worried you," she said, "but I didn't know what else to do."

"Don't fret about it, Betsy," Mrs. Jeffries said. "We all occasionally have to make a decision. You did the best you could."

"We'll git over our scare," Luty said. "I'm just glad you're all right."

"All's well that ends well," Hatchet agreed.

"Thank goodness you're 'ome in one piece," Wiggins said. "That's 'ow I feel about it."

"I'll fix you a nice hot cuppa cocoa to make up for all the runnin' about you've had to do today," Mrs. Goodge said.

Smythe just glared at her.

Mrs. Jeffries met the inspector when he came in the front door. Within minutes, she had him in the drawing room, a glass of sherry in hand.

"I'll only have a quick one." He yawned. "I'm really very tired. It's been a most distressing day."

"You look exhausted, sir," she told him, clucking her tongue sympathetically. "How did the investigation go today?"

The inspector told her everything. By the time he put down his second glass of Harveys and got to his feet, Mrs. Jeffries knew every detail of the day's events.

The inspector went up to bed and Mrs. Jeffries

double-checked that the front door was locked. As she climbed the stairs to her own room, she was deep in thought. She quite admired the way the inspector had decided not to arrest Arthur Grant. Like her employer, she didn't see him as the murderer either. But then, who had done it?

She went into her room and walked over to the window. The darkness blanketed her softly as she sat down in the chair and stared out into the night.

Mrs. Jeffries let her mind float free. Bits and pieces of conversations, facts and clues popped in and out of her consciousness willy-nilly. She made no move to sort anything, to categorize or to analyze. She'd already done that with no success whatsover. For a long time, she sat staring out at the London night. This case was absurdly muddled. Nothing was coming to her, nothing at all.

She sat up straighter in her chair and marshalled her thoughts. Perhaps, after all, she ought to try thinking about it in a more rational manner.

"Hadn't you better hurry, sir?" Mrs. Jeffries asked anxiously. The others were due to come by for a meeting this morning, and if she didn't get the inspector out of the house and on his way, their schedule would be thrown off completely. There were any number of things that she wanted to take care of today. Why, her little session in the dark last night had come up with half a dozen things that needed clarifying. "It's almost nine o'clock."

The inspector speared the last bite of egg with his fork. "Oh, I've plenty of time," he replied. "Constable Barnes is picking me up here and not at the station." He eyed the last piece of toast in the rack consideringly and then reached for it.

"Would you care for more tea, sir?" she asked. She cocked her head as she heard a faint knock on the front door. A moment later, footsteps sounded in the hallway, and Constable Barnes was ushered in by Betsy.

"Good morning, Inspector, Mrs. Jeffries." He nodded politely to both of them.

"Good morning," Witherspoon said. "Do sit down, Constable, and have a cup of tea."

"Thank you, sir." Barnes took a chair. "I believe I will."

Mrs. Jeffries poured him a cup and placed it in front of him. She was rather annoyed, but, of course, would never let it show. But now she had both of them camped out in the dining room and Luty and Hatchet would be here any minute. Perhaps if she began clearing up the breakfast things. Turning, she reached for the empty tray from the sideboard.

"We got an answer to our inquiry, sir," Barnes said to Witherspoon. "The police in Kent searched his cottage. There's lots of paintings there, but none that fit the description we gave 'em of the Caldararos."

Mrs. Jeffries picked up the tray and slowly,

250

slowly turned back to the table.

"Gracious," the inspector said. "That was quick."

"Not really, sir," Barnes replied. "You see, they'd already been to Underhill's house. They'd searched it when we notifed them he'd been murdered."

Mrs. Jeffries put the tray down on the end of the table.

"Yes, yes, of course," Witherspoon muttered. He looked at his housekeeper. "Gracious, you're trying to clear up and we're in your way."

"Not at all, sir," she said hastily. "Do take your time."

"Where on earth could those paintings have got to?" Witherspoon said plaintively. "They couldn't have just disappeared into thin air."

Barnes smiled slyly. "Well, sir, I think we might have an answer to that question. Seems they've got a fairly bright young copper down in Kent. After our telegram askin' about the paintings, he took it upon himself to start askin' a few questions. Seems on the day before the murder a local delivery van was seen going to the Underhill cottage. He took a large parcel away with him."

Witherspoon brightened considerably. Now they were getting somewhere. "Where did he take it?"

"He took it, as instructed, to the train station and gave it to the station master." Barnes took a quick sip of tea. "The station master put it on the next train for London and it arrived that day, sir."

"Then Underhill must have picked it up and taken it somewhere other than his lodgings."

"But that's just it, sir," Barnes said. "He didn't. The parcel wasn't picked up till the next day — the day that Underhill was killed."

"Perhaps he got it early in the day, before he went to the Grant house?" the inspector suggested.

"No, sir. He didn't. That's why I was a bit late, sir. I nipped along to Victoria myself this morning and had a chat with the clerk in the freight office. That parcel got picked up late in the afternoon on the day of the murder. The clerk remembers it clearly. It was fetched by a footman in uniform. That means it was picked up after Underhill was already dead."

Mrs. Jeffries went absolutely still. Something niggled at the back of her mind. Something someone had said, something mentioned casually and then forgotten. For she knew instinctively that these misplaced paintings were the key to why James Underhill had been murdered.

Chapter 11

"Are you going to arrest Arthur Grant?" Mrs. Jeffries asked the inspector.

"I'm afraid I must," the inspector replied. He and Barnes both got to their feet.

"But what about the parcel, sir?" she asked. She knew he was getting ready to make a big mistake. "You said yourself that these missing paintings were the key to finding Underhill's killer."

"I did?" Witherspoon's brows rose. "Really? When?"

"Last night, sir," Mrs. Jeffries said hastily. She fervently hoped that between his exhaustion and the sherry, he wouldn't remember precisely what all he'd said. "Right before you retired for the night, sir. You said, 'Mark my words, Mrs. Jeffries, those Caldararos are the key to this.' Well, sir, as you've so brilliantly deduced, the missing paintings are probably in that parcel."

Witherspoon smiled fondly at his housekeeper. She was so very devoted to him. Obviously, she hung on his every word. Quite fortunate that she did too. He couldn't remember all that much about last night. He'd been dead tired. "Yes, well, I do believe I'm right, Mrs. Jeffries," he said. "The missing paintings are the key to this whole business. But as the constable has just told us, the parcel is gone."

Mrs. Jeffries almost lost her nerve. If she was wrong, she'd be making a terrible fool of herself and worse, making an even bigger one of the inspector. An error at this junction could ruin everything. But if she did nothing, then the evidence — the only real evidence of the crime — could be destroyed.

"I know, sir," she said slowly. "But surely you know how to find it. Oh please, sir. Do let me in on it. Do let me see if I'm right."

"Pardon?"

She stared at him for a moment. "Oh, dear. I'm so sorry, sir. I quite forgot myself." She threw her hand up in a supplicating gesture. "I know you can't really tell me what you've planned. Please forgive my boldness, sir. I'm afraid I got carried away. I know I'm just your housekeeper, just a silly woman . . ."

"Really, Mrs. Jeffries," Witherspoon said in alarm. "You're not in the least silly and you're not just my housekeeper — you're a very valued friend. Er . . . what uh . . . what kind of plan did you think I had in mind?"

Mrs. Jeffries glanced at Barnes. She was treading on thin ice here, very thin ice indeed. The constable was no fool. But when their gazes met, the only thing she saw in his eyes was a faint amusement and perhaps, just perhaps, a bit of admiration.

"Well, sir, I naturally assumed you'd carry on along the lines of what we discussed last night." She smiled innocently. "You know, when we were talking about your list of suspects and how everyone, but most especially Arthur Grant, all needed Underhill alive and not dead." They had mentioned that aspect of the case, but only in passing.

"Yes, I recall saying that." Witherspoon nodded encouragingly.

"And you also mentioned that no one at the Grant house could remember letting Underhill into the house that day," she continued. "Well — I mean, it's quite obvious, isn't it, sir? There's only one person who could have let him in, and that person deliberately met him at the door, deliberately ushered him inside before any of the servants could answer the door. That person then searched his pockets and found the freight bill for the parcel. Having done that, that person gave the freight bill to a footman with instructions to pick up the parcel and take it somewhere safe."

Witherspoon stared at her in amazement. "I'm afraid I don't recall saying any of that," he admitted. But the idea did make a bizarre kind of sense. If a servant had answered the door, they'd have taken the man's coat and hung it up. But none of them had done it. Yet someone had hung Underhill's overcoat up in the cloakroom. Furthermore, in this investigation, there was only one household with a uniformed footman in it.

"You didn't say it, sir," she said briskly, "but you certainly implied it during our chat last night." She snatched up the tray. "But perhaps I misunderstood . . ."

"No, no, Mrs. Jeffries," Witherspoon said quickly. "I didn't mean any such thing."

She gave him a cheerful smile, praying he'd understand what the next obvious step might be. She couldn't push any further. "Thank you, sir. I'm glad I'm not completely wrong in these things. I do rather like to think I've learned a bit from you, sir."

"If I might make a suggestion, sir," Barnes said softly. "I think that before we arrest Arthur Grant, we might have a word with the footman at the Grant house."

Mrs. Jeffries gave the constable a dazzling smile.

"Would you pass me the jam pot, please?" Betsy asked Smythe. She didn't really want any. It was just an excuse to speak to him. Except for a grunt or two when she'd said goodnight before going up to bed last night, he'd not spoken to her. Betsy thought he was being awfully silly, but it bothered her nonetheless.

Wordlessly, he pushed the earthenware bowl in front of Betsy's plate.

"Thank you," she said. He grunted in reply.

"You're not in a 'appy mood this mornin', are

ya?" Wiggins asked the coachman. He looked up as the housekeeper flew into the kitchen.

"Quick," she said, looking at Wiggins. "I want you to follow the inspector to the Grant house. Don't let him see you, but stay with him. He may go somewhere else. Go with him if he does, but do stay out of sight."

"I'll get the carriage," Smythe offered. "If he's on the move, he may try to grab a hansom. I'll make sure I'm there instead. I can always tell 'im I was takin' Bow and Arrow out for their exercise and 'appened to be passin'.."

She was touched by their faith in her. Neither man bothered asking questions. They simply got up and prepared to do precisely what she'd asked. If she was wrong, she'd feel awful. Worse, she'd feel as though she'd let them down. "Excellent idea, Smythe," she said.

"Is things comin' to a head, then?" Mrs. Goodge asked eagerly. "Is there goin' to be an arrest?"

"Either that," Mrs. Jeffries admitted, "or I've made the world's worst mistake."

The footman wasn't a man at all, but a lad who looked to be about sixteen. His name was Horace Weatherby. Dark haired, pale skinned and small for his age, he stood next to a locked cupboard in the butler's pantry and stared at the inspector out of wary, pale blue eyes. "Mrs. Grant said you wanted to see me, sir?" he began. "But I can't think why. I wasn't even here when that Mr. Underhill got himself murdered."

"We know that," the inspector assured him. "We understand that you'd been sent out on an errand. Is that correct?"

"That's right," Horace replied.

"Where was this errand?" Witherspoon asked kindly. He knew what the butler had told him the boy had been sent to do, but he wanted to hear it from the lad's own mouth.

"I went to take Miss Collier's book back to Mudies Library," he replied.

"But according to the butler, you were gone for several hours," Barnes said. "Mudies is only over on New Oxford Street. Surely it didn't take that long to get there and back. Now why don't you tell us the truth? You went somewhere else that day, didn't you?"

Panic crossed the lad's face. "I'm not supposed to tell," he whined. "It'll cost me my job, ya know. She told me she'd sack me if I told anyone."

"This is murder you're involved in, lad," Barnes said sternly. "So you'd best tell us the truth."

"Murder," he squawked. "I didn't have nothin' to do with that. I just done what she told me and went to the station to get that parcel."

"Where did you take it?" Witherspoon pressed. "Did you bring it back here?"

"All I did was what she told me." He twisted his hands together. "I picked it up at Victoria, hopped a hansom and took it to the Great

Northern Railway booking office."

"Is the parcel still there?" Barnes asked.

"I think so," he sputtered. "She ain't hardly left the house. Not since the murder, not since you coppers have been all over the place."

"Sit down, Hepzibah," Luty said calmly. "You're goin' to walk a hole in the floor."

"But what if I'm wrong?" Mrs. Jeffries suppressed a shudder. "What if I'm completely off the mark and the inspector is making a fool of himself at this very moment?"

"He's not makin' a fool of himself," Mrs. Goodge declared stoutly. She flopped a cut of veal onto the chopping block and began trimming off the fat. "He's a smart man, our inspector."

"But what if my reasoning is faulty?" She closed her eyes and wished she could turn back the clock. She'd sent them off on the flimsiest of evidence. Yet this morning, in one of those tremendous flashes of insight that make one so very certain, she'd been sure she was right. "It wouldn't be the first time I'd been wrong."

"No," Hatchet agreed. "But in all the cases we've solved, you've been correct far more often than you've been wrong. Besides, you've explained your reasoning to us. I think it makes perfect sense. As a matter of fact, I congratulate you on seeing what should have been obvious to all of us from the start."

"So do I," Betsy said. "Like you told us, every

one of the others had a good reason for wanting Underhill alive." She held up her hand and began ticking off the fingers. "First, Arthur Grant needed him to get the original Caldararos back so his father'd not disinherit him when he found out the ones on his wall were fakes. Lydia Modean needed him alive so she could get the photographic plate back, Helen Collier wanted to marry him and Neville Grant and Tyrell Modean didn't have a reason to want him dead. That only leaves one person."

"It was lucky Smythe happened to be driving up Holland Park Road when we were trying to find a hansom," Barnes said dryly.

"Oh, there was nothing in the least lucky about it," Witherspoon said. He leaned forward on the seat and dropped his voice, though with the rattle of the carriage and the noise of the horses it would be impossible for anyone to overhear him. "Smythe deliberately drove up this way," he said conspiratorially. "My staff are always so very keen to learn whatever they can about my cases. They're always hanging about when I'm out on the hunt. I pretend not to notice. Though I must admit, having them about has come in handy a time or two. But as I said, I pretend not to notice them. I don't wish to make them feel awkward. I know they only do it because they're devoted to me. That, of course, and a very mild case of well . . . shall we say, hero worship."

"That's very good of you, sir," Barnes said.

"Not at all." Witherspoon waved his hand. "I'm a very fortunate man. Not many people have a staff as loyal and devoted as mine."

Barnes smiled. "That's true, sir. You are a very lucky man."

The carriage pulled around the corner into Lower Regent Street. Witherspoon leaned out the window, trying to gauge how far they were from the Great Northern Railway booking office.

"I don't like the fact that she left the house right after sending the footman in to see us," Barnes commented. He scanned the pavement on the other side of the carriage.

"Yes, it's a pity it was her and not the butler who opened the front door," Witherspoon replied soberly. "We'd no choice but to ask her to send the footman to us. I do hope we didn't give the game away."

"Well, sir, we'll know if we get there and the freight clerk tells us the parcel was picked up just a few minutes earlier by a woman matching her description," Barnes said. "She'll not be able to get far. Not lugging a bloomin' great package."

The carriage pulled up in front of the booking office and the two policemen got out. Smythe stayed atop the carriage, ever alert and at the ready. Wiggins, who'd told the inspector he'd tagged along for the ride, jumped down and stood impatiently by the lamppost on the corner, eager to see what would happen next.

"I'll go in, shall I?" Barnes started for the door

of the booking office.

"We'll both go . . ." Witherspoon paused, his eyes narrowing as his attention was caught by something on the other side of the carriage. "Gracious, there she is!" He pointed at the pedestrian island in the middle of the road. "We're too late. She's got the parcel. Quick, Barnes, come on. She's getting in a hansom."

He started across the road, only to be halted in his tracks by someone yanking hard on his jacket from behind. "Gracious," the inspector yelped just as an oncoming carriage thundered past.

"Sorry, sir," Wiggins said, "but that coach was comin' so fast I didn't think you'd 'ave time to get out of the way."

"Thank you, my boy," the inspector said gratefully. "I was in such a hurry, I wasn't paying attention to where I was going. If you'd not grabbed me, I'd have been crushed."

"Oh look, sir," Barnes cried. "She's gettin' away."

They watched in dismay as the hansom took off down the road.

Smythe whipped up the reins and in moments had turned the inspector's carriage around. "Hop in, sir," he called. "We can catch up."

Wiggins jumped on and scrambled up beside the coachman while the inspector and Barnes leapt inside. "I don't think we've a hope of catching her," the constable complained. "And if she manages to get rid of those paintings, we've no evidence." Actually, Barnes wasn't sure even catching her with the parcel would lead to anything. He hadn't a clue as to what was going on, but he was sure the inspector did.

Witherspoon stuck his head out the window. "I can see the hansom. We'll catch her, all right," he called. "Smythe is an excellent driver."

They raced through the busy London streets as fast as they dared. In what seemed like minutes to Barnes, but was in reality a bit longer than that, they'd covered well over a mile. From out the window, the murky waters of the Thames lay just ahead.

Smythe, using every ounce of skill and ingenuity at his command, kept the hansom in sight, but couldn't manage to get close enough to get directly behind it.

"The hansom's stopped," the inspector shouted, pointing ahead toward the water.

"She's gettin' out, sir," Wiggins cried.

Barnes stuck his head out and saw the hansom pulling away and a woman, a parcel clutched in her hands, racing for the side of the river. "She's goin' to toss it, sir," he warned.

But Smythe had seen too. Whistling through his teeth, he spurred his horses on even faster. They raced for the embankment. He didn't pull up. He didn't even slow. He simply kept on going right up to the concrete buttresses that held back the waters of the Thames.

She saw them as they jumped out of the carriage.

Instead of tossing the parcel over the edge of

the embankment, she turned and started running along the pavement, the parcel clutched under her arm.

They started after her. The inspector was in the lead, but Wiggins was by far the fastest. "I'll get her," he called as he flew past the two policemen. But fast as he was, he didn't gain on her very quickly.

Driven by fear, she was a good deal swifter than one would expect from a woman of her age and background.

Wiggins put on more speed.

"Stop in the name of the law," Witherspoon gasped, but she paid no attention. She just kept running.

Wiggins finally began to gain on her. She looked back over her shoulder and saw him closing the gap between them. He was now only twenty or so yards away. She stopped and threw the parcel over the buttress.

"Oh, no," Wiggins cried as he saw it disappear over the side. He skidded to a halt beside her. She stared at him stonily, but didn't try to run. Wiggins was grateful for that. He wasn't quite sure what to do. Luckily, Barnes got there a second later, and right on his heels was the inspector.

"Out for a walk, Inspector?" she said calmly.

"Mary Grant," he replied breathlessly, "you're under arrest for the murder of James Underhill."

She smiled then. "But you won't be able to

prove it, will you? And by the time you drag the Thames and find those paintings, the water will have ruined your precious evidence, I'm afraid. Even an expert won't be able to help you then."

"We won't have to drag the river," Wiggins said cheerfully. He pointed toward the river. "Look, there's a barge moored right below us. The parcel's sittin' right atop of it plain as the nose on yer face."

It was well past ten o'clock by the time the inspector got home that night. When he came into the kitchen he wasn't in the least surprised to see his entire household, as well as Luty and Hatchet, sitting at the table.

"Good evening, sir," Mrs. Jeffries said cheerfully. "Luty and Hatchet happened to drop by after supper, sir. Once they heard about all your excitement this afternoon, they were determined to stay and hear what happened."

"I don't mind in the least," he said. He reached down and patted Fred on the head. "There's a good boy, now. Just be a patient fellow and I'll take you walkies after I've had a cup of tea."

"Do tell us everything," Mrs. Jeffries urged him. She poured him a cup of steaming hot tea. "What happened?"

"Well, luckily, as I'm sure Wiggins told you, the parcel didn't go in the water." He picked up his cup and took a sip. "We took it back to the station and opened it and, of course, the Caldararos were inside." He winced. "It was at this point that I almost made a dreadful mistake, you see. Fortunately, Constable Barnes had the good sense to send for the Modeans. They came at once and brought their art expert with them." He shook his head. "It's a very good thing he did too. Otherwise, I'd have arrested the right person but the motive would have been all wrong and then she'd never have confessed."

"She confessed?" Mrs. Jeffries said.

"Oh, yes," the inspector said, "as soon as we brought in the art expert and the other set of Caldararos, the ones she'd sent out to be cleaned. We'd got those too, you see. So both sets were at the station. As soon as she saw all that, she told us everything."

"Ya gonna tell us why she murdered Underhill?" Luty demanded.

"To stop him from selling the original Caldararos back to Arthur Grant," Witherspoon explained. "Mary Grant knew all about how Arthur had sold the ones she'd brought to the marriage — the ones she'd used for a dowry — to Underhill. That was fine by her too. The last things she wanted was Underhill bringing those back to be authenticated."

"But why?" Betsy asked. "If they was the ones she brung to the marriage, why would she want Underhill to have them?"

"She didn't. But she didn't want an art expert authenticating them either," Witherspoon said. "You see, they were forgeries too. But, of course, that's where I'd made my mistake. I thought she'd murdered Underhill because she was angry at him."

"Angry at him?" Mrs. Goodge repeated.

"Oh, yes. I thought she'd poisoned him because she was in love with him. Gracious, I oughtn't to admit this, but I really had got it wrong. I thought that's why she refused to admit to us that her sister was going to marry Underhill. She was in love with him herself."

"But sir," Mrs. Jeffries asked softly, "if she murdered him out of jealousy, why would she have wanted to get her hands on the parcel so badly?"

Witherspoon gave an embarrassed shrug. "I thought those paintings belonged to her sister, Helen Collier. It occurred to me that Mary Grant had bought herself a husband with her paintings so why shouldn't her sister?"

"All right, Hepzibah," Luty said as soon as the inspector had taken Fred outside. "Tell us how ya figured it out."

"As I told you earlier, no one seemed to really benefit from Underhill's death," she explained. "No one liked him very much, but most of them weren't better off with the man dead. I couldn't see how anyone benefitted from his death except Irene Simmons. But she was completely out of the picture as she'd disappeared well before he ate those fatal mints. Last night, when the inspector told me that the poison had been found under Arthur's mattress, I realized that the mints must have been tampered with that very day. That meant that Irene and Morante couldn't have done the killing."

"But 'ow'd ya figure it was her?" Smythe asked.

"I wasn't sure until this morning," Mrs. Jeffries said. "It was when the constable told us about the parcel coming up by train from Underhill's cottage in Kent that it all fell into place. I understood then that there was only one thing that could be in that package — the paintings. The ones Arthur Grant had paid Underhill to give him back. Then I asked myself who wouldn't want the original paintings back — after all, if the originals were back in place and authenticated, the sale could go through and the Grants could pay off their creditors. Then I realized that Underhill might have been murdered to stop that from taking place. But why? Who would benefit from those paintings not being authenticated? There could be only one person. The person who'd originally brought them into the Grant household. Mary Grant. She didn't want an expert seeing them because she knew they were fakes. She knew they were worthless. And she'd do anything, anything at all, to make sure her husband never found out."

"But the ones she sent out to be cleaned were fakes as well," Betsy said.

"But that worked to her advantage," Mrs. Jeffries pointed out. "Once Neville Grant found out what his son had done, he'd disinherit him.

That was one of the things she wanted. Her husband is a very sick man. He probably won't live much longer. He has nothing of value except his art collection. An art collection of real paintings she wanted to inherit. I'll wager Mary Grant knew full well what Arthur had done. She probably encouraged James Underhill to set up the whole scheme. The last thing she wanted was Underhill sending her paintings back here. If it ever came out that she'd bought her way into this marriage with forged paintings, Neville Grant would have divorced her in an instant." She smiled quickly at the cook. "We found out from Mrs. Goodge's excellent sources that Mr. Grant wasn't adverse to divorce. He was on the verge of divorcing his first wife, Arthur's mother, before she so conveniently died."

"Cor blimey." Wiggins gazed at her in admiration. "You're really somethin'. Figurin' all that out with just a few bits and pieces."

"Don't give me too much credit," she told him. "Without the information all of you worked so hard to get, we'd have never discovered the truth. Don't forget, Wiggins, it was you who told us about the footman who wasn't at the house on the afternoon of the murder. That was on the day when you were sure you'd not found out anything worthwhile and that turned out to be a vital clue."

"But how did you know that Mrs. Grant had searched Underhill's pockets?" Betsy asked.

"I was guessing there," she said. "But I remembered how the inspector had told me that none of the servants could recall letting Underhill into the house that day." She faltered a bit and hoped she wasn't blushing. "And, well, I've done the same thing myself with the inspector."

"Mrs. Jeffries, you're goin' all red in the cheeks," Wiggins pointed out.

Luty snickered. "Met him at the door so you could search his pockets, huh?"

"Only because I needed to borrow his spectacles," she explained. "You know, for when we need a good excuse to go to the station or the scene of the crime the next day. But that's what made me think that might be what happened. When you want to have a good look through someone's pockets, you make sure you get to the door before the butler does."

"Absolutely, madam," Hatchet concurred. "No self-respecting butler would let the lady of the house take a gentleman's coat."

They talked about the case for another half hour, until the inspector, with a very tired Fred at his heels, came in from his walk and went up to bed.

Luty and Hatchet said their good nights after promising to come back the next morning for the delightful task of reliving the case from start to finish. Mrs. Jeffries went to make sure the back door was locked, Wiggins took Fred up to his room and Mrs. Goodge started to clear the table.

"I'll do that," Betsy volunteered. "You and Mrs. Jeffries go on to bed. I can tidy up."

"Thanks, dear," the cook said gratefully as she headed for her room. "I'll tell Mrs. Jeffries you're finishin' up down here. She could do with a good night's sleep herself."

Betsy cleaned off the table, rinsed out the cups and saucers and emptied the last of the tea down the drain.

She'd just reached over to turn down the lamp when she heard footsteps on the stairs. "Oh, it's you. I thought you'd gone to bed."

"I come down to see if you needed any 'elp," Smythe said. "It didn't seem fair for you to 'ave to do all the tidyin' up."

"I don't mind." Betsy picked up the small lantern the household used at night.

"Betsy, I'm sorry I've been so . . . so . . ."

"Cold?" she supplied. "Is that the word you're lookin' for?"

"I didn't mean it," he said, desperate to make things up with her. "But I was so scared when ya didn't come 'ome, lass. It took me a day or two to get over it."

She stared at him in the semidarkness. The way he'd acted towards her had hurt her feelings. Hurt her worse than she'd like to admit, and one part of her wanted to get him back. But on the other hand, she hated being at odds with him.

"Look, I know you're right annoyed with me," he began.

"I'm not annoyed anymore," she interrupted. "I can even understand a bit how you felt. I wouldn't like walkin' the floor and worrying myself sick over you, either."

He broke into a broad grin.

"But I've done it a time or two and I've not treated you like you've got the plague just because you made me a bit anxious."

He spread his hands helplessly. "I said I was sorry."

"I don't want you making a habit of this," she warned, raising her hand to stop him. "The next time I might not be so forgiving."

"I won't," he promised. He reached for the lantern. " 'Ere, let me get that for ya. Would you like to go out with me tomorrow?"

"Out where?" But it was a silly question. She'd go anywhere with him.

"To the photographic exhibit at the Crystal Palace," he said, taking her elbow and heading for the hall. "But there's just one thing."

"What's that?" she asked.

"We have to take Wiggins with us."